BEWARE.

REAL WITCHES dress in ordinary clothes
and look like ordinary women.
BUT THEY ARE NOT ORDINARY.
They are always plotting and scheming
with murderous, bloodthirsty
thoughts – and they **HATE CHILDREN.**

THE GRAND HIGH WITCH
hates children most of all and plans to
make every single one of YOU disappear.

Only **ONE BOY** and his **GRANDMOTHER**
can stop her, but if their plan fails
THE GRAND HIGH WITCH
will frizzle them like fritters,
and then what . . . ?

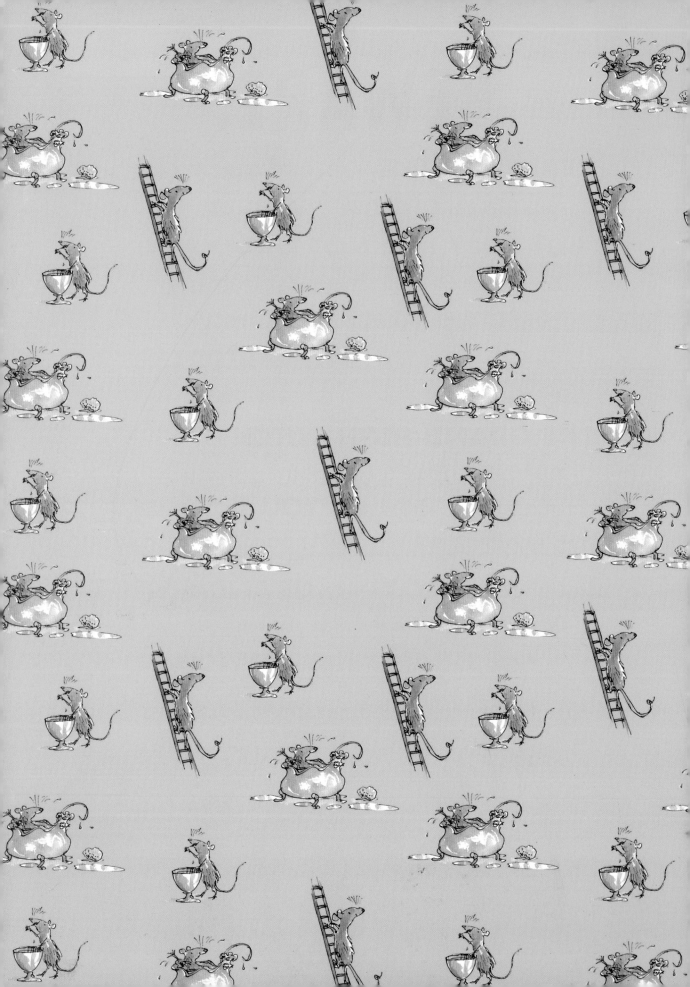

HOW MANY HAVE YOU READ?

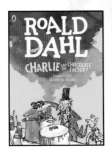     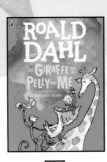

☐ ☐ ☐ ☐ ☐ ☐

   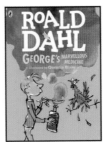  

☐ ☐ ☐ ☐ ☐ ☐

  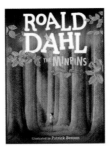  

☐ ☐ ☐ ☐ ☐

MORE THAN 5? WHOOPSEY-SPLUNKERS! You've got some reading to do!

MORE THAN 10? More tremendous things await – keep turning those pages.

ALL OF THEM? Whoopee! Which was your favourite?

ROALD DAHL was a spy, ace fighter pilot, chocolate historian and medical inventor. He was also the author of *Charlie and the Chocolate Factory*, *Matilda*, *The BFG* and many more brilliant stories. He remains THE WORLD'S NUMBER ONE STORYTELLER.

QUENTIN BLAKE has illustrated more than three hundred books and was Roald Dahl's favourite illustrator. In 1980 he won the prestigious Kate Greenaway Medal. In 1999 he became the first ever Children's Laureate and in 2013 he was knighted for services to illustration.

ROALD DAHL

THE WITCHES

Illustrated by Quentin Blake

PUFFIN

Find out more about Roald Dahl by visiting
the website at roalddahl.com

PUFFIN BOOKS

UK | USA | Canada | Ireland | Australia
India | New Zealand | South Africa

Puffin Books is part of the Penguin Random House group of companies
whose addresses can be found at global.penguinrandomhouse.com.

www.penguin.co.uk   www.puffin.co.uk   www.ladybird.co.uk

Penguin
Random House
UK

First published by Jonathan Cape 1983
Published by Puffin Books 1985
Colour edition published 2017
003

Printed and bound in China

A CIP catalogue record for this book is available from the British Library

ISBN: 978–0–141–34517–8

All correspondence to:
Puffin Books, Penguin Random House Children's
80 Strand, London WC2R 0RL

~ For Liccy ~

CONTENTS

Chapter One

A Note About Witches

In fairy-tales, witches always wear silly black hats and black cloaks, and they ride on broomsticks.

But this is not a fairy-tale. This is about REAL WITCHES.

The most important thing you should know about REAL WITCHES is this. Listen very carefully. Never forget what is coming next.

REAL WITCHES dress in ordinary clothes and look very much like ordinary women. They live in ordinary houses and they work in ORDINARY JOBS.

That is why they are so hard to catch.

A REAL WITCH hates children with a red-hot sizzling hatred that is more sizzling and red-hot than any hatred you could possibly imagine.

A REAL WITCH spends all her time plotting to get rid of the children in her particular territory. Her passion is to do away with them, one by one. It is all she thinks about the whole day long. Even if she is working as a cashier in a supermarket or typing letters for a businessman or driving round in a fancy car (and she could be doing any of these things), her mind will always be plotting and scheming and churning and burning and whizzing and phizzing with murderous bloodthirsty thoughts.

'Which child,' she says to herself all day long, 'exactly which child shall I choose for my next squelching?'

A REAL WITCH gets the same pleasure from squelching a child as *you* get from eating a plateful of strawberries and thick cream.

She reckons on doing away with one child a week. Anything less than that and she becomes grumpy.

One child a week is fifty-two a year.

Squish them and squiggle them and make them disappear.

That is the motto of all witches.

Very carefully a victim is chosen. Then the witch stalks the wretched child like a hunter stalking a little bird in the forest. She treads softly. She moves quietly. She gets closer and closer. Then at last, when everything is ready . . . *phwisst!* . . . and she swoops! Sparks fly. Flames leap. Oil boils. Rats howl. Skin shrivels. And the child disappears.

A witch, you must understand, does not knock children on the head or stick knives into them or shoot at them with a pistol. People who do those things get caught by the police.

A witch never gets caught. Don't forget that she has magic in her fingers and devilry dancing in her blood. She can make stones jump

about like frogs and she can make tongues of flame go flickering across the surface of the water.

These magic powers are very frightening.

Luckily, there are not a great number of REAL WITCHES in the world today. But there are still quite enough to make you nervous. In England, there are probably about one hundred of them altogether. Some countries have more, others have not quite so many. No country in the world is completely free from WITCHES.

A witch is always a woman.

I do not wish to speak badly about women. Most women are lovely. But the fact remains that all witches *are* women. There is no such thing as a male witch.

On the other hand, a ghoul is always a male. So indeed is a barghest. Both are dangerous. But neither of them is half as dangerous as a REAL WITCH.

As far as children are concerned, a REAL WITCH is easily the most dangerous of all the living creatures on earth. What makes her doubly dangerous is the fact that she doesn't *look* dangerous. Even when you know all the secrets (you will hear about those in a minute), you can still never be quite sure whether it is a witch you are gazing at or just a kind lady. If a tiger were able to make himself look like a large dog with a waggy tail, you would probably go up and pat him on the head. And that would be the end of you. It is the same with witches. They all look like nice ladies.

Kindly examine the picture on the next page. Which lady is the witch? That is a difficult question, but it is one that every child must try to answer.

For all you know, a witch might be living next door to you right now.

Or she might be the woman with the bright eyes who sat opposite you on the bus this morning.

She might be the lady with the dazzling smile who offered you a sweet from a white paper bag in the street before lunch.

She might even – and this will make you jump – she might even be your lovely school-teacher who is reading these words to you at this very moment. Look carefully at that teacher. Perhaps she is smiling at the absurdity of such a suggestion. Don't let that put you off. It could be part of her cleverness.

I am not, of course, telling you for one second that your teacher actually is a witch. All I am saying is that she *might* be one. It is most unlikely. But – and here comes the big 'but' – *it is not impossible.*

Oh, if only there were a way of telling for sure whether a woman was a witch or not, then we could round them all up and put them in the meat-grinder. Unhappily, there is no such way. But there *are* a number of little signals you can look out for, little quirky habits that all witches have in common, and if you know about these, if you remember them always, then you might just possibly manage to escape from being squelched before you are very much older.

Chapter Two

MY GRANDMOTHER

I myself had two separate encounters with witches before I was eight years old. From the first I escaped unharmed, but on the second occasion I was not so lucky. Things happened to me that will probably make you scream when you read about them. That can't be helped. The truth must be told. The fact that I am still here and able to speak to you (however peculiar I may look) is due entirely to my wonderful grandmother.

My grandmother was Norwegian. The Norwegians know all about witches, for Norway, with its black forests and icy mountains, is where the first witches came from. My father and my mother were also Norwegian, but because my father had a business in England, I had been born there and had lived there and had started going to an English school. Twice a year, at Christmas and in the summer, we went back to Norway to visit my grandmother. This old lady, as far as I could gather, was just about the only surviving relative we had on either side of our family. She was my mother's mother and I absolutely adored her. When she and I were together we spoke in either Norwegian or in English. It didn't matter which. We were equally fluent in both languages, and I have to admit that I felt closer to her than to my mother.

Soon after my seventh birthday, my parents took me as usual to spend Christmas with my grandmother in Norway. And it was over there, while my father and mother and I were driving in icy weather just north of Oslo, that our car skidded off the road and went

tumbling down into a rocky ravine. My parents were killed. I was firmly strapped into the back seat and received only a cut on the forehead.

I won't go into the horrors of that terrible afternoon. I still get the shivers when I think about it. I finished up, of course, back in my grandmother's house with her arms around me tight and both of us crying the whole night long.

'What are we going to do now?' I asked her through the tears.

'You will stay here with me,' she said, 'and I will look after you.'

'Aren't I going back to England?'

'No,' she said. 'I could never do that. Heaven shall take my soul, but Norway shall keep my bones.'

The very next day, in order that we might both try to forget our great sadness, my grandmother started telling me stories. She was a wonderful story-teller and I was enthralled by everything she told me. But I didn't become really excited until she got on to the subject of witches. She was apparently a great expert on these creatures and she made it very clear to me that her witch stories, unlike most of the others, were not imaginary tales. They were all true. They were the *gospel* truth. They were history. Everything she was telling me about witches had actually happened and I had better believe it. What was worse, what was far, far worse, was that witches were still with us. They were all around us and I had better believe that, too.

'Are you *really* being truthful, Grandmamma? *Really* and *truly* truthful?'

'My darling,' she said, 'you won't last long in this world if you don't know how to spot a witch when you see one.'

'But you told me that witches look like ordinary women, Grandmamma. So how can I spot them?'

'You must listen to me,' my grandmother said. 'You must remember everything I tell you. After that, all you can do is cross your heart and pray to heaven and hope for the best.'

We were in the big living-room of her house in Oslo and I was ready for bed. The curtains were never drawn in that house, and through the windows I could see huge snowflakes falling slowly on to an outside world that was as black as tar. My grandmother was tremendously old and wrinkled, with a massive wide body which was smothered in grey lace. She sat there majestic in her armchair, filling every inch of it. Not even a mouse could have squeezed in to sit beside her. I myself, just seven years old, was crouched on the floor at her feet, wearing pyjamas, dressing-gown and slippers.

'You swear you aren't pulling my leg?' I kept saying to her. 'You swear you aren't just pretending?'

'Listen,' she said, 'I have known no less than five children who have simply vanished off the face of this earth, never to be seen again. The witches took them.'

'I still think you're just trying to frighten me,' I said.

'I am trying to make sure you don't go the same way,' she said. 'I love you and I want you to stay with me.'

'Tell me about the children who disappeared,' I said.

My grandmother was the only grandmother I ever met who smoked cigars. She lit one now, a long black cigar that smelt of burning rubber. 'The first child I knew who disappeared,' she said, 'was called Ranghild Hansen. Ranghild was about eight at the time, and she was playing with her little sister on the lawn. Their mother, who was baking bread in the kitchen, came outside for a breath of air. "Where's Ranghild?" she asked.

' "She went away with the tall lady," the little sister said.

' "What tall lady?" the mother said.

' "The tall lady in white gloves," the little sister said. "She took Ranghild by the hand and led her away." No one,' my grandmother said, 'ever saw Ranghild again.'

'Didn't they search for her?' I asked.

'They searched for miles around. Everyone in the town helped, but they never found her.'

'What happened to the other four children?' I asked.

'They vanished just as Ranghild did.'

'How, Grandmamma? How did they vanish?'

'In every case a strange lady was seen outside the house, just before it happened.'

'But how did they vanish?' I asked.

'The second one was very peculiar,' my grandmother said. 'There was a family called Christiansen. They lived up on

Holmenkollen, and they had an old oil-painting in the living-room which they were very proud of. The painting showed some ducks in the yard outside a farmhouse. There were no people in the painting, just a flock of ducks on a grassy farmyard and the farmhouse in the background. It was a large painting and rather pretty. Well, one day their daughter Solveg came home from school eating an apple. She said a nice lady had given it to her on the street. The next morning little Solveg was not in her bed. The parents searched everywhere but they couldn't find her. Then all of a sudden her father shouted, "There she is! That's Solveg feeding the ducks!" He was pointing at the oil-painting, and sure enough Solveg was in it. She was standing in the farmyard in the act of throwing bread to the ducks out of a basket. The father rushed up to the painting and touched her. But that didn't help. She was simply a part of the painting, just a picture painted on the canvas.'

'Did *you* ever see that painting, Grandmamma, with the little girl in it?'

'Many times,' my grandmother said. 'And the peculiar thing was that little Solveg kept changing her position in the picture. One day she would actually be inside the farmhouse and you could see her face looking out of the window. Another day she would be far over to the left with a duck in her arms.'

'Did you see her moving in the picture, Grandmamma?'

'Nobody did. Wherever she was, whether outside feeding the ducks or inside looking out of the window, she was always motionless, just a figure painted in oils. It was all very odd,' my grandmother said. 'Very odd indeed. And what was most odd of all was that as the years went by, she kept growing older in the picture. In ten years, the small girl had become a young woman. In thirty years, she was middle-aged. Then all at once, fifty-four years after it all happened, she disappeared from the picture altogether.'

'You mean she died?' I said.

'Who knows?' my grandmother said. 'Some very mysterious things go on in the world of witches.'

'That's two you've told me about,' I said. 'What happened to the third one?'

'The third one was little Birgit Svenson,' my grandmother said. 'She lived just across the road from us. One day she started growing feathers all over her body. Within a month, she had turned into a large white chicken. Her parents kept her for years in a pen in the garden. She even laid eggs.'

'What colour eggs?' I said.

'Brown ones,' my grandmother said. 'Biggest eggs I've ever seen in my life. Her mother made omelettes out of them. Delicious they were.'

I gazed up at my grandmother, who sat there like some ancient

queen on her throne. Her eyes were misty-grey and they seemed to be looking at something many miles away. The cigar was the only real thing about her at that moment, and the smoke it made billowed round her head in blue clouds.

'But the little girl who became a chicken didn't disappear?' I said.

'No, not Birgit. She lived on for many years laying her brown eggs.'

'You said all of them disappeared.'

'I made a mistake,' my grandmother said. 'I am getting old. I can't remember everything.'

'What happened to the fourth child?' I asked.

'The fourth was a boy called Harald,' my grandmother said. 'One morning his skin went all greyish-yellow. Then it became hard and crackly, like the shell of a nut. By evening, the boy had turned to stone.'

'Stone?' I said. 'You mean real stone?'

'Granite,' she said. 'I'll take you to see him if you like. They still keep him in the house. He stands in the hall, a little stone statue.

Visitors lean their umbrellas up against him.'

Although I was very young, I was not prepared to believe everything my grandmother told me. And yet she spoke with such conviction, with such utter seriousness, and with never a smile on her face or a twinkle in her eye, that I found myself beginning to wonder.

'Go on, Grandmamma,' I said. 'You told me there were five altogether. What happened to the last one?'

'Would you like a puff of my cigar?' she said.

'I'm only seven, Grandmamma.'

'I don't care what age you are,' she said. 'You'll never catch a cold if you smoke cigars.'

'What about number five, Grandmamma?'

'Number five,' she said, chewing the end of her cigar as though it were a delicious asparagus, 'was rather an interesting case. A nine-year-old boy called Leif was summer-holidaying with his family on the fjord, and the whole family was picnicking and swimming off some rocks on one of those little islands. Young Leif dived into the water and his father, who was watching him, noticed that he stayed under for an unusually long time. When he came to the surface at last, he wasn't Leif any more.'

'What was he, Grandmamma?'

'He was a porpoise.'

'He wasn't! He couldn't have been!'

'He was a lovely young porpoise,' she said. 'And as friendly as could be.'

'Grandmamma,' I said.

'Yes, my darling?'

'Did he really and truly turn into a porpoise?'

'Absolutely,' she said. 'I knew his mother well. She told me all about it. She told me how Leif the Porpoise stayed with them all that afternoon giving his brothers and sisters rides on his back. They had a wonderful time. Then he waved a flipper at them and swam away, never to be seen again.'

'But Grandmamma,' I said, 'how did they know that the porpoise was actually Leif?'

'He talked to them,' my grandmother said. 'He laughed and joked with them all the time he was giving them rides.'

'But wasn't there a most tremendous fuss when this happened?' I asked.

'Not much,' my grandmother said. 'You must remember that here in Norway we are used to that sort of thing. There are witches everywhere. There's probably one living in our street this very moment. It's time you went to bed.'

'A witch wouldn't come in through my window in the night, would she?' I asked, quaking a little.

'No,' my grandmother said. 'A witch will never do silly things like climbing up drainpipes or breaking into people's houses. You'll be quite safe in your bed. Come along. I'll tuck you in.'

Chapter Three

How to Recognize a Witch

The next evening, after my grandmother had given me my bath, she took me once again into the living-room for another story.

'Tonight,' the old woman said, 'I am going to tell you how to recognize a witch when you see one.'

'Can you always be sure?' I asked.

'No,' she said, 'you can't. And that's the trouble. But you can make a pretty good guess.'

She was dropping cigar ash all over her lap, and I hoped she wasn't going to catch on fire before she'd told me how to recognize a witch.

'In the first place,' she said, 'a REAL WITCH is certain always to be wearing gloves when you meet her.'

'Surely not *always*,' I said. 'What about in the summer when it's hot?'

'Even in the summer,' my grandmother said. 'She has to. Do you want to know why?'

'Why?' I said.

'Because she doesn't have finger-nails. Instead of finger-nails, she has thin curvy claws, like a cat, and she wears the gloves to hide them. Mind you, lots of very respectable women wear gloves, especially in winter, so this doesn't help you very much.'

'Mamma used to wear gloves,' I said.

'Not in the house,' my grandmother said. 'Witches wear gloves

16

even in the house. They only take them off when they go to bed.'

'How do you know all this, Grandmamma?'

'Don't interrupt,' she said. 'Just take it all in. The second thing to remember is that a REAL WITCH is always bald.'

'*Bald?*' I said.

'Bald as a boiled egg,' my grandmother said.

I was shocked. There was something indecent about a bald woman. 'Why are they bald, Grandmamma?'

'Don't ask me why,' she snapped. 'But you can take it from me that not a single hair grows on a witch's head.'

'How horrid!'

'Disgusting,' my grandmother said.

'If she's bald, she'll be easy to spot,' I said.

'Not at all,' my grandmother said. 'A REAL WITCH always wears a wig to hide her baldness. She wears a first-class wig. And it is almost impossible to tell a really first-class wig from ordinary hair unless you give it a pull to see if it comes off.'

'Then that's what I'll have to do,' I said.

'Don't be foolish,' my grandmother said. 'You can't go round pulling at the hair of every lady you meet, even if she *is* wearing gloves. Just you try it and see what happens.'

'So that doesn't help much either,' I said.

'None of these things is any good on its own,' my grandmother said. 'It's only when you put them all together that they begin to make a little sense. Mind you,' my grandmother went on, 'these wigs do cause a rather serious problem for witches.'

'What problem, Grandmamma?'

'They make the scalp itch most terribly,' she said. 'You see, when an actress wears a wig, or if you or I were to wear a wig, we would be putting it on over our own hair, but a witch has to put it straight on to her naked scalp. And the underneath of a wig is always very rough and scratchy. It sets up a frightful itch on the bald skin. It causes nasty sores on the head. Wig-rash, the witches call it. And it doesn't half itch.'

'What other things must I look for to recognize a witch?' I asked.

'Look for the nose-holes,' my grandmother said. 'Witches have slightly larger nose-holes than ordinary people. The rim of each nose-hole is pink and curvy, like the rim of a certain kind of sea-shell.'

'Why do they have such big nose-holes?' I asked.

'For smelling with,' my grandmother said. 'A REAL WITCH has the most amazing powers of smell. She can actually smell out a child who is standing on the other side of the street on a pitch-black night.'

'She couldn't smell me,' I said. 'I've just had a bath.'

'Oh yes she could,' my grandmother said. 'The cleaner you happen to be, the more smelly you are to a witch.'

'That can't be true,' I said.

'An absolutely clean child gives off the most ghastly stench to a witch,' my grandmother said. 'The dirtier you are, the less you smell.'

'But that doesn't make sense, Grandmamma.'

'Oh yes it does,' my grandmother said. 'It isn't the *dirt* that the witch is smelling. It is *you*. The smell that drives a witch mad actually comes right out of your own skin. It comes oozing out of your skin in waves, and these waves, stink-waves the witches call them, go floating through the air and hit the witch right smack in her nostrils. They send her reeling.'

'Now wait a minute, Grandmamma . . .'

'Don't interrupt,' she said. 'The point is this. When you haven't washed for a week and your skin is all covered over with dirt, then quite obviously the stink-waves cannot come oozing out nearly so strongly.'

'I shall never have a bath again,' I said.

'Just don't have one too often,' my grandmother said. 'Once a month is quite enough for a sensible child.'

It was at moments like these that I loved my grandmother more than ever.

'Grandmamma,' I said, 'if it's a dark night, how can a witch smell the difference between a child and a grown-up?'

'Because grown-ups don't give out stink-waves,' she said. 'Only children do that.'

'But I don't *really* give out stink-waves, do I?' I said. 'I'm not giving them out at this very moment, am I?'

'Not to me you aren't,' my grandmother said. 'To me you are smelling like raspberries and cream. But to a witch you would be smelling absolutely disgusting.'

'What would I be smelling of?' I asked.

'Dogs' droppings,' my grandmother said.

I reeled. I was stunned. '*Dogs' droppings!*' I cried. 'I am *not* smelling of dogs' droppings! I don't believe it! I *won't* believe it!'

'What's more,' my grandmother said, speaking with a touch of relish, 'to a witch you'd be smelling of *fresh* dogs' droppings.'

'That simply is not true!' I cried. 'I know I am not smelling of dogs' droppings, stale or fresh!'

'There's no point in arguing about it,' my grandmother said. 'It's a fact of life.'

I was outraged. I simply couldn't bring myself to believe what my grandmother was telling me.

'So if you see a woman holding her nose as she passes you in the street,' she went on, 'that woman could easily be a witch.'

I decided to change the subject. 'Tell me what else to look for in a witch,' I said.

'The eyes,' my grandmother said. 'Look carefully at the eyes, because the eyes of a REAL WITCH are different from yours and mine. Look in the middle of each eye where there is normally a little black dot. If she is a witch, the black dot will keep changing colour, and you will see fire and you will see ice dancing right in the very centre of the coloured dot. It will send shivers running all over your skin.'

My grandmother leaned back in her chair and sucked away contentedly at her foul black cigar. I squatted on the floor, staring up at her, fascinated. She was not smiling. She looked deadly serious.

'Are there other things?' I asked her.

'Of course there are other things,' my grandmother said. 'You don't seem to understand that witches are not actually women at all. They *look* like women. They talk like women. And they are able to act like women. But in actual fact, they are totally different animals. They are demons in human shape. That is why they have claws and bald heads and queer noses and peculiar eyes, all of which they have to conceal as best they can from the rest of the world.'

'What else is different about them, Grandmamma?'

'The feet,' she said. 'Witches never have toes.'

'No toes!' I cried. 'Then what do they have?'

'They just have feet,' my grandmother said. 'The feet have square ends with no toes on them at all.'

'Does that make it difficult to walk?' I asked.

'Not at all,' my grandmother said. 'But it does give them a problem with their shoes. All ladies like to wear small rather pointed shoes, but a witch, whose feet are very wide and square at the ends, has the most awful job squeezing her feet into those neat little pointed shoes.'

'Why doesn't she wear wide comfy shoes with square ends?' I asked.

'She dare not,' my grandmother said. 'Just as she hides her baldness with a wig, she must also hide her ugly witch's feet by squeezing them into pretty shoes.'

'Isn't that terribly uncomfortable?' I said.

'Extremely uncomfortable,' my grandmother said. 'But she has to put up with it.'

'If she's wearing ordinary shoes, it won't help me to recognize her, will it, Grandmamma?'

'I'm afraid it won't,' my grandmother said. 'You might possibly see her limping very slightly, but only if you were watching closely.'

'Are those the only differences then, Grandmamma?'

'There's one more,' my grandmother said. 'Just one more.'

'What is it, Grandmamma?'

'Their spit is blue.'

'Blue!' I cried. 'Not blue! Their spit can't be *blue*!'

'Blue as a bilberry,' she said.

'You don't mean it, Grandmamma! Nobody can have blue spit!'

'Witches can,' she said.

'Is it like ink?' I asked.

'Exactly,' she said. 'They even use it to write with. They use those old-fashioned pens that have nibs and they simply lick the nib.'

'Can you *notice* the blue spit, Grandmamma? If a witch was talking to me, would I be able to notice it?'

'Only if you looked carefully,' my grandmother said. 'If you looked very carefully you would probably see a slight bluish tinge on her teeth. But it doesn't show much.'

'It would if she spat,' I said.

'Witches never spit,' my grandmother said. 'They daren't.'

I couldn't believe my grandmother would be lying to me. She went to church every morning of the week and she said grace before every meal, and somebody who did that would never tell lies. I was beginning to believe every word she spoke.

'So there you are,' my grandmother said. 'That's about all I can tell you. None of it is very helpful. You can still never be absolutely sure whether a woman is a witch or not just by looking at her. But if she is wearing the gloves, if she has the large nose-holes, the queer eyes and the hair that looks as though it might be a wig, and if she has a bluish tinge on her teeth – if she has all of these things, then you run like mad.'

'Grandmamma,' I said, 'when you were a little girl, did *you* ever meet a witch?'

'Once,' my grandmother said. 'Only once.'

'What happened?'

'I'm not going to tell you,' she said. 'It would frighten you out of your skin and give you bad dreams.'

'Please tell me,' I begged.

'No,' she said. 'Certain things are too horrible to talk about.'

'Does it have something to do with your missing thumb?' I asked.

Suddenly, her old wrinkled lips shut tight as a pair of tongs and the hand that held the cigar (which had no thumb on it) began to quiver very slightly.

I waited. She didn't look at me. She didn't speak. All of a sudden she had shut herself off completely. The conversation was finished.

'Goodnight, Grandmamma,' I said, rising from the floor and kissing her on the cheek.

She didn't move. I crept out of the room and went to my bedroom.

Chapter Four

THE GRAND HIGH WITCH

The next day, a man in a black suit arrived at the house carrying a brief-case, and he held a long conversation with my grandmother in the living-room. I was not allowed in while he was there, but when at last he went away, my grandmother came in to me, walking very slowly and looking very sad.

'That man was reading me your father's will,' she said.

'What is a will?' I asked her.

'It is something you write before you die,' she said. 'And in it you say who is going to have your money and your property. But most important of all, it says who is going to look after your child if both the mother and father are dead.'

A fearful panic took hold of me. 'It did say you, Grandmamma?' I cried. 'I don't have to go to somebody else, do I?'

'No,' she said. 'Your father would never have done that. He has asked me to take care of you for as long as I live, but he has also asked that I take you back to your own house in England. He wants us to stay there.'

'But why?' I said. 'Why can't we stay here in Norway? You would hate to live anywhere else! You told me you would!'

'I know,' she said. 'But there are a lot of complications with money and with the house that you wouldn't understand. Also, it said in the will that although all your family is Norwegian, you were born in England and you have started your education there and he wants you to continue going to English schools.'

'Oh, Grandmamma!' I cried. '*You* don't want to go and live in our English house, I know you don't!'

'Of course I don't,' she said. 'But I am afraid I must. The will said that your mother felt the same way about it, and it is important to respect the wishes of the parents.'

There was no way out of it. We had to go to England, and my grandmother started making arrangements at once. 'Your next school term begins in a few days,' she said, 'so we don't have any time to waste.'

On the evening before we left for England, my grandmother got on to her favourite subject once again. 'There are not as many witches in England as there are in Norway,' she said.

'I'm sure I won't meet one,' I said.

'I sincerely hope you won't,' she said, 'because those English witches are probably the most vicious in the whole world.'

As she sat there smoking her foul cigar and talking away, I kept looking at the hand with the missing thumb. I couldn't help it. I was fascinated by it and I kept wondering what awful thing had happened that time when she had met a witch. It must have been something absolutely appalling and gruesome otherwise she would have told me about it. Maybe the thumb had been twisted off. Or perhaps she had been forced to jam her thumb down the spout of a boiling kettle until it was steamed away. Or did someone pull it out of her hand like a tooth? I couldn't help trying to guess.

'Tell me what those English witches do, Grandmamma,' I said.

'Well,' she said, sucking away at her stinking cigar, 'their favourite ruse is to mix up a powder that will turn a child into some creature or other that all grown-ups hate.'

'What sort of a creature, Grandmamma?'

'Often it's a slug,' she said. 'A slug is one of their favourites. Then the grown-ups step on the slug and squish it without knowing it's a child.'

'That's perfectly beastly!' I cried.

'Or it might be a flea,' my grandmother said. 'They might turn you into a flea, and without realizing what she was doing your own mother would get out the fleapowder and then it's goodbye you.'

'You're making me nervous, Grandmamma. I don't think I want to go back to England.'

'I've known English witches,' she went on, 'who have turned children into pheasants and then sneaked the pheasants up into the woods the very day before the pheasant-shooting season opened.'

'Owch,' I said. 'So they get shot?'

'Of course they get shot,' she said. 'And then they get plucked and roasted and eaten for supper.'

I pictured myself as a pheasant flying frantically over the men with the guns, swerving and dipping as the guns exploded below me.

'Yes,' my grandmother said, 'it gives the English witches great pleasure to stand back and watch the grown-ups doing away with their own children.'

'I really don't want to go to England, Grandmamma.'

'Of course you don't,' she said. 'Nor do I. But I'm afraid we've got to.'

'Are witches different in every country?' I asked.

'Completely different,' my grandmother said. 'But I don't know much about the other countries.'

'Don't you even know about America?' I asked.

'Not really,' she answered. 'Although I have heard it said that over there the witches are able to make the grown-ups eat their own children.'

'Never!' I cried. 'Oh no, Grandmamma! That couldn't be true!'

'I don't know whether it's true or not,' she said. 'It's only a rumour I've heard.'

'But how could they possibly make them eat their own children?' I asked.

'By turning them into hot-dogs,' she said. 'That wouldn't be too difficult for a clever witch.'

'Does every single country in the world have its witches?' I asked.

'Wherever you find people, you find witches,' my grandmother said. 'There is a Secret Society of Witches in every country.'

'And do they all know one another, Grandmamma?'

'They do not,' she said. 'A witch only knows the witches in her own country. She is strictly forbidden to communicate with any foreign witches. But an English witch, for example, will know all the other witches in England. They are all friends. They ring each other up. They swap deadly recipes. Goodness knows what else they talk about. I hate to think.'

I sat on the floor, watching my grandmother. She put her cigar stub in the ashtray and folded her hands across her stomach. 'Once a year,' she went on, 'the witches of each separate country hold their own secret meeting. They all get together in one place to receive a lecture from The Grand High Witch Of All The World.'

'From *who*?' I cried.

'She is the ruler of them all,' my grandmother said. 'She is all-powerful. She is without mercy. All other witches are petrified of her. They see her only once a year at their Annual Meeting. She goes there to whip up excitement and enthusiasm, and to give orders. The Grand High Witch travels from country to country attending these Annual Meetings.'

'Where do they have these meetings, Grandmamma?'

'There are all sorts of rumours,' my grandmother answered. 'I have heard it said that they just book into a hotel like any other group of women who are holding a meeting. I have also heard it said that some very peculiar things go on in the hotels they stay in. It is rumoured that the beds are never slept in, that there are burn marks on the bedroom carpets, that toads are discovered in the bathtubs, and that down in the kitchen the cook once found a baby crocodile swimming in his saucepan of soup.'

My grandmother picked up her cigar and took another puff, inhaling the foul smoke deeply into her lungs.

'Where does The Grand High Witch live when she's at home?' I asked.

'Nobody knows,' my grandmother said. 'If we knew that, then she could be rooted out and destroyed. Witchophiles all over the world have spent their lives trying to discover the secret headquarters of The Grand High Witch.'

'What is a witchophile, Grandmamma?'

'A person who studies witches and knows a lot about them,' my grandmother said.

'Are you a witchophile, Grandmamma?'

'I am a retired witchophile,' she said. 'I am too old to be active any longer. But when I was younger, I travelled all over the globe trying to track down The Grand High Witch. I never came even close to succeeding.'

'Is she rich?' I asked.

'She's rolling,' my grandmother said. 'Simply rolling in money. Rumour has it that there is a machine in her headquarters which is exactly like the machine the government uses to print the bank-notes you and I use. After all, bank-notes are only bits of paper with special designs and pictures on them. Anyone can make them who has the right machine and the right paper. My guess is that The Grand High Witch makes all the money she wants and she dishes it out to witches everywhere.'

'What about foreign money?' I asked.

'Those machines can make *Chinese* money if you want them to,' my grandmother said. 'It's only a question of pressing the right button.'

'But Grandmamma,' I said, 'if nobody has ever seen The Grand High Witch, how can you be so sure she exists?'

My grandmother gave me a long and very severe look. 'Nobody has ever seen the Devil,' she said, 'but we know he exists.'

The next morning, we sailed for England and soon I was back in the old family house in Kent, but this time with only my grandmother to look after me. Then the Easter Term began and every weekday I went to school and everything seemed to have come back to normal again.

Now at the bottom of our garden there was an enormous conker tree, and high up in its branches Timmy (my best friend) and I had started to build a magnificent tree-house. We were able to work on it only at the weekends, but we were getting along fine. We had begun with the floor, which we built by laying wide planks between two quite far-apart branches and nailing them down. Within a month, we had finished the floor. Then we

constructed a wooden railing around the floor and that left only the roof to be built. The roof was the difficult bit.

One Saturday afternoon when Timmy was in bed with flu, I decided to make a start on the roof all by myself. It was lovely being high up there in that conker tree, all alone with the pale young leaves coming out everywhere around me. It was like being in a big green cave. And the height made it extra exciting. My grandmother had told me that if I fell I would break a leg, and every time I looked down, I got a tingle along my spine.

I worked away, nailing the first plank on the roof. Then suddenly, out of the corner of my eye, I caught sight of a woman standing immediately below me. She was looking up at me and smiling in the most peculiar way. When most people smile, their lips go out sideways. This woman's lips went upwards and downwards, showing all her front teeth and gums. The gums were like raw meat.

It is always a shock to discover that you are being watched when you think you are alone.

And what was this strange woman doing in our garden anyway?

I noticed that she was wearing a small black hat and she had black gloves on her hands and the gloves came nearly up to her elbows.

Gloves! She was wearing *gloves*!

I froze all over.

'I have a present for you,' she said, still staring at me, still smiling, still showing her teeth and gums.

I didn't answer.

'Come down out of that tree, little boy,' she said, 'and I shall give you the most exciting present you've ever had.' Her voice had a curious rasping quality. It made a sort of metallic sound, as though her throat was full of drawing-pins.

Without taking her eyes from my
face, she very slowly put one
of those gloved hands
into her purse and
drew out a small
green snake.
She held it up
for me to see.

'It's tame,'
she said.

The snake began
to coil itself around her forearm.
It was brilliant green.

'If you come down here, I shall give him
to you,' she said.

Oh Grandmamma, I thought, come and help me!

Then I panicked. I dropped the hammer and shot up that
enormous tree like a monkey. I didn't stop until I was as high as
I could possibly go, and there I stayed, quivering with fear.

I couldn't see the woman now. There were layers and layers of leaves between her and me.

I stayed up there for hours and I kept very still. It began to grow dark. At last, I heard my grandmother calling my name.

'I'm up here,' I shouted back.

'Come down at once!' she called out. 'It's past your suppertime.'

'Grandmamma!' I shouted. 'Has that woman gone?'

'What woman?' my grandmother called back.

'The woman in the black gloves!'

There was silence from below. It was the silence of somebody who was too stunned to speak.

'Grandmamma!' I shouted again. '*Has she gone?*'

'Yes,' my grandmother answered at last. 'She's gone. I'm here, my darling. I'll look after you. You can come down now.'

I climbed down. I was trembling. My grandmother enfolded me in her arms. 'I've seen a witch,' I said.

'Come inside,' she said. 'You'll be all right with me.'

She led me into the house and gave me a cup of hot cocoa with lots of sugar in it. 'Tell me everything,' she said.

I told her.

By the time I had finished, it was my grandmother who was trembling. Her face was ashy grey and I saw her glance down at that hand of hers that didn't have a thumb. 'You know what this means,' she said. 'It means that there is one of them in our district. From now on I'm not letting you walk alone to school.'

'Do you think she could be after me specially?' I asked.

'No,' she said. 'I doubt that. One child is as good as any other to those creatures.'

It is hardly surprising that after that I became a very witch-conscious little boy. If I happened to be alone on the road and saw a woman approaching who was wearing gloves, I would quickly skip across to the other side. And as the weather remained pretty cold during the whole of that month, nearly *everybody* was wearing gloves. Curiously enough though, I never saw the woman with the green snake again.

That was my first witch. But it wasn't my last.

Chapter Five

SUMMER HOLIDAYS

The Easter holidays came and went, and the Summer Term began at school. My grandmother and I had already planned to take our summer holiday in Norway and we talked about almost nothing else every evening. She had booked a cabin for each of us on the boat from Newcastle to Oslo at the earliest possible moment after my school broke up, and from Oslo she was going to take me to a place she knew down on the south coast near Arendal where she had spent her own summer holidays as a child nearly eighty years ago.

'All day long,' she said, 'my brother and I were out in the rowing-boat. The whole coast is dotted with tiny islands and there's nobody on them. We used to explore them and dive into the sea off the lovely smooth granite rocks, and sometimes on the way out we would drop the anchor and fish for cod and whiting, and if we caught anything we would build a fire on an island and fry the fish in a pan for our lunch. There is no finer fish in the world than absolutely fresh cod.'

'What did you use for bait, Grandmamma, when you went fishing?'

'Mussels,' she said. 'Everyone uses mussels for bait in Norway. And if we didn't catch any fish, we would boil the mussels in a saucepan and eat those.'

'Were they good?'

'Delicious,' she said. 'Cook them in sea-water and they are tender and salty.'

'What else did you do, Grandmamma?'

'We used to row out and wave to the shrimp-boats on their way home, and they would stop and give us a handful of shrimps each. The shrimps were still warm from having been just cooked, and we would sit in the rowing-boat peeling them and gobbling them up. The head was the best part.'

'The head?' I said.

'You squeeze the head between your teeth and suck out the inside. It's marvellous. You and I will do all those things this summer, my darling,' she said.

'Grandmamma,' I said, 'I can't wait. I simply can't wait to go.'

'Nor can I,' she said.

When there were only three weeks of the Summer Term left, an awful thing happened. My grandmother got pneumonia. She became very ill, and a trained nurse moved into the house to look after her. The doctor explained to me that pneumonia is not normally a dangerous illness nowadays because of penicillin, but when a person is more than eighty years old, as my grandmother was, then it is very dangerous indeed. He said he didn't even dare to move her to hospital in her condition, so she stayed in her bedroom and I hung about outside the door while oxygen cylinders and all sorts of other frightening things were taken in to her.

'Can I go in and see her?' I asked.

'No, dear,' the nurse said. 'Not at the moment.'

A fat and jolly lady called Mrs Spring, who used to come and clean our house every day, also moved in and slept in the house. Mrs Spring looked after me and cooked my meals. I liked her very much, but she wasn't a patch on my grandmother for telling stories.

One evening, about ten days later, the doctor came downstairs

and said to me, 'You can go in and see her now, but only for a short time. She's been asking for you.'

I flew up the stairs and burst into my grandmother's room and threw myself into her arms.

'Hey there,' the nurse said. 'Be careful with her.'

'Will you be all right now, Grandmamma?' I asked.

'The worst is over,' she said. 'I'll soon be up again.'

'Will she?' I said to the nurse.

'Oh yes,' the nurse answered, smiling. 'She told us she simply had to get better because she had to look after you.'

I gave her another hug.

'They won't let me have a cigar,' she said. 'But you wait till they're gone.'

'She's a tough old bird,' the nurse said. 'We'll have her up in another week.'

The nurse was right. Within a week, my grandmother was thumping around the house with her gold-topped cane and interfering with Mrs Spring's cooking. 'I thank you for all your help, Mrs Spring,' she said, 'but you can go home now.'

'Oh no I can't,' Mrs Spring said. 'Doctor told me to see that you take it very easy for the next few days.'

The doctor said more than that. He dropped a bombshell on my grandmother and me by telling us that on no account were we to risk the journey to Norway this summer.

'Rubbish!' my grandmother cried. 'I've promised him we'll go!'

'It's too far,' the doctor said. 'It would be very dangerous. But I'll tell you what you *can* do. You can take your grandson to a nice hotel on the south coast of England instead. The sea air is just what you need.'

'Oh no!' I said.

'Do you want your grandmother to die?' the doctor asked me.

'Never!' I said.

'Then don't let her go on a long journey this summer. She's not yet strong enough. And stop her smoking those vile black cigars.'

In the end, the doctor had his way about the holiday, but not about the cigars. Rooms were booked for us in a place called the Hotel Magnificent in the famous seaside town of Bournemouth. Bournemouth, my grandmother told me, was full of old people like herself. They retired there by the thousand because the air was so bracing and healthy it kept them, so they believed, alive for a few extra years.

'Does it?' I asked.

'Of course not,' she said. 'It's tommyrot. But just for once I think we've got to obey the doctor.'

Soon after that, my grandmother and I took the train to Bournemouth and settled into the Hotel Magnificent. It was an enormous white building on the sea-front and it looked to me like a pretty boring place to spend a summer holiday in. I had my own separate bedroom, but there was a door connecting my room with my grandmother's room so that we could visit each other without going into the corridor.

Just before we left for Bournemouth, my grandmother had given me, as consolation, a present of two white mice in a little cage and of course I took them with me. They were terrific fun, those mice. I called them William and Mary, and in the hotel I set out right away teaching them to do tricks.

The first trick I taught them was to creep up the sleeve of my jacket and come out by my neck.

Then I taught them to climb up the back of my neck on to the top of my head. I did this by putting cake crumbs in my hair.

On the very first morning after our arrival, the chambermaid was making my bed when one of my mice poked its head out from under the sheets. The maid let out a shriek that brought a dozen people running to see who was being murdered. I was reported to the Manager. There followed an unpleasant scene in the Manager's office with the Manager, my grandmother and me.

The Manager, whose name was Mr Stringer, was a bristly man in a black tail-coat. 'I cannot permit mice in my hotel, madam,' he said to my grandmother.

'How dare you say that when your rotten hotel is full of rats anyway!' my grandmother cried.

'Rats!' cried Mr Stringer, going mauve in the face. 'There are no rats in this hotel!'

'I saw one this very morning,' my grandmother said. 'It was running down the corridor into the kitchen!'

'That is not true!' cried Mr Stringer.

'You had better get the rat-catcher in at once,' my grandmother said, 'before I report you to the Public Health Authorities. I expect there's rats scuttling all over the kitchen floor and stealing the food off the shelves and jumping in and out of the soup!'

'Never!' cried Mr Stringer.

'No wonder my breakfast toast was all nibbled round the edges this morning,' my grandmother went on relentlessly. 'No wonder it had a nasty ratty taste. If you're not careful, the Health people will be ordering the entire hotel to be closed before everyone gets typhoid fever.'

'You are not being serious, madam,' Mr Stringer said.

'I was never more serious in my life,' my grandmother said. 'Are you or are you not going to allow my grandson to keep his white mice in his room?'

The Manager knew when he was beaten. 'May I suggest a compromise, madam?' he said. 'I will permit him to keep them in his room as long as they are never allowed out of the cage. How's that?'

'That will suit us very well,' my grandmother said, and she stood up and marched out of the room with me behind her.

There is no way you can train mice inside a cage. Yet I dared not let them out because the chambermaid was spying on me all the time. She had a key to my door and she kept bursting in at all hours, trying to catch me with the mice out of the cage. She told me that the first mouse to break the rules would be drowned in a bucket of water by the hall-porter.

I decided to seek a safer place where I could carry on with the training. There must surely be an empty room in this enormous hotel. I put one mouse into each trouser-pocket and wandered downstairs in search of a secret spot.

The ground floor of the hotel was a maze of public rooms, all of them named in gold letters on the doors. I wandered through 'The Lounge' and 'The Smoking-Room' and 'The Card-Room' and 'The Reading-Room' and 'The Drawing-Room'. None of them was empty. I went down a long wide corridor and at the end of it I came to 'The Ballroom'. There were double-doors leading into it, and in front of the doors there was a large notice-board on a stand. The notice on the board said,

RSPCC MEETING

STRICTLY PRIVATE

THIS ROOM IS RESERVED

FOR THE

ANNUAL MEETING

OF

THE ROYAL SOCIETY

FOR THE PREVENTION

OF CRUELTY TO CHILDREN

The double-doors into the room were open. I peeped in. It was a colossal room. There were rows and rows of chairs, all facing a platform. The chairs were painted gold and they had little red cushions on the seats. But there was not a soul in sight.

I sidled cautiously into the room. What a lovely secret silent place it was. The meeting of the Royal Society for the Prevention of Cruelty to Children must have taken place earlier in the day, and now they had all gone home. Even if they hadn't, even if they *did* suddenly come pouring in, they would be wonderful kind people who would look with favour upon a young

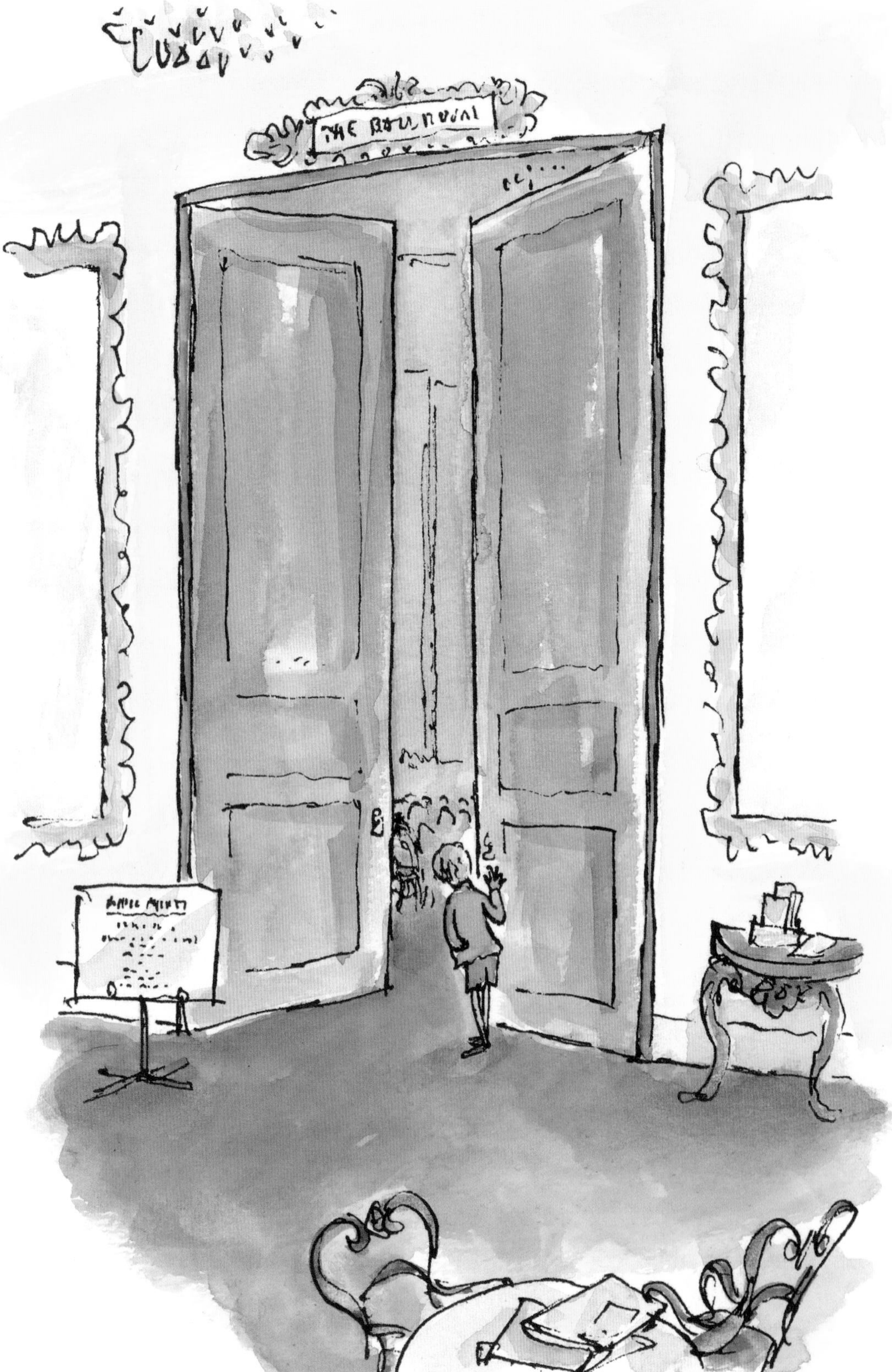

mouse-trainer going about his business.

At the back of the room there was a large folding screen with Chinese dragons painted on it. I decided, just to be on the safe side, to go behind this screen and do my training there. I wasn't a bit frightened of the Prevention of Cruelty to Children people, but there was always a chance that Mr Stringer, the Manager, might pop his head round the door. If he did and if he saw the mice, the poor things would be in the hall-porter's bucket of water before I could shout stop.

I tiptoed to the back of the room and settled myself on the thick green carpet behind the big screen. What a splendid place this was! Ideal for mouse-training! I took William and Mary out of my trouser-pockets. They sat beside me on the carpet, quiet and well-behaved. The trick I was going to teach them today was tight-rope walking. It is not all that difficult to train an intelligent mouse to be an expert tight-rope walker provided you know exactly how to go about it. First, you must have a piece of string. I had that. Then you must have some good cake. A fine currant cake is the favourite food of white mice. They are dotty about it. I had brought with me a rock cake which I had pocketed while having tea with Grandmamma the day before.

Now here's what you do. You stretch the string tight between your two hands, but you start by keeping it very short, only about three inches. You put the mouse on your right hand and a little piece of cake on your left hand. The mouse is therefore only three inches away from the cake. He can see it and he can smell it. His whiskers twitch with excitement. He can almost reach the cake by leaning forward, but not quite. He only has to take two steps along the string to reach this tasty morsel. He ventures forward, one paw on the string, then the other. If the mouse has a good sense of balance, and most of them have, he will get across easily. I started with William. He walked the string without a moment's hesitation. I let him have a quick nibble of the cake just to whet his appetite. Then I put him back on my right hand.

This time I lengthened the string. I made it about six inches long. William knew what to do now. With superb balance, he walked step by step along the string until he reached the cake. He was rewarded with another nibble.

Quite soon, William was walking a twenty-four-inch tight-rope

(or rather tight-string) from one hand to the other to reach the cake. It was wonderful to watch him. He was enjoying himself tremendously. I was careful to hold the string near the carpet so that if he did lose his balance, he wouldn't have far to fall. But he never fell. William was obviously a natural acrobat, a great tight-rope-walking mouse.

Now it was Mary's turn. I put William on the carpet beside me and rewarded him with some extra crumbs and a currant. Then I started going through the same routine all over again with Mary. My blinding ambition, you see, my dream of dreams, was to become one day the owner of a White Mouse Circus. I would have a small stage with red curtains in front of it, and when the curtains were drawn apart, the audience would see my world-famous performing mice walking on tight-ropes, swinging from trapezes, turning somersaults in the air, bouncing on trampolines and all the rest of it. I would have white mice riding on white rats, and the rats would gallop furiously round and round the stage. I was beginning to picture myself travelling first-class all over the globe with my Famous White Mouse Circus, and performing before all the crowned heads of Europe.

I was about halfway through Mary's training when suddenly I heard voices outside the Ballroom door. The sound grew louder. It swelled into a great babble of speech from many throats. I recognized the voice of the awful Hotel Manager, Mr Stringer.

Help, I thought.

But thank heavens for the huge screen.

I crouched behind it and peered through the crack between two of the folding sections. I could see the entire length and width of the Ballroom without anyone seeing me.

'Well, ladies, I am sure you will be quite comfortable in here,'

Mr Stringer's voice was saying. Then in through the double-doors he marched, black tail-coat and all, spreading his arms wide as he ushered in a great flock of ladies. 'If there is anything we can do for you, do not hesitate to let me know,' he went on. 'Tea will be served for all of you on the Sunshine Terrace after you have concluded your meeting.' With that, he bowed and scraped himself out of the room as a vast herd of ladies from the Royal Society for the Prevention of Cruelty to Children came streaming in. They wore pretty clothes and all of them had hats on their heads.

Chapter Six

THE MEETING

Now that the Manager had gone, I was not particularly alarmed. What better than to be imprisoned in a room full of these splendid ladies? If I ever got talking to them, I might even suggest that they come and do a bit of cruelty-to-children preventing at my school. We could certainly use them there.

In they came, talking their heads off. They began milling round and choosing their seats, and there was a whole lot of stuff like, 'Come and sit next to me, Millie dear,' and, 'Oh, hel-*lo*, Beatrice! I haven't seen you since the last meeting! What an adorable dress you have on!'

I decided to stay where I was and let them get on with their meeting while I got on with my mouse-training, but I watched them for a while longer through the crack in the screen, waiting for them to settle down. How many were there? I guessed about two hundred. The back rows filled up first. They all seemed to want to sit as far back from the platform as possible.

There was a lady wearing a tiny green hat in the middle of the back row who kept scratching the nape of her neck. She couldn't leave it alone. It fascinated me the way her fingers kept scratching away at the hair on the back of her neck. Had she known somebody was watching her from behind, I'm sure she would have been embarrassed. I wondered if she had dandruff. All of a sudden, I noticed that the lady next to her was doing the same thing!

And the next one!

And the next!

The whole lot of them were doing it. They were all scratching away like mad at the hair on the backs of their necks!

Did they have fleas in their hair?

More likely it was nits.

A boy at school called Ashton had had nits in his hair last term and the matron had made him dip his whole head in turpentine. It killed the nits all right, but it nearly killed Ashton as well. Half the skin came away from his scalp.

I began to be fascinated by these hair-scratching ladies. It is always funny when you catch someone doing something coarse and she thinks no one is looking. Nose-picking, for example, or scratching her bottom. Hair-scratching is very nearly as unattractive, especially if it goes on and on.

I decided it had to be nits.

Then the most astonishing thing happened. I saw one lady pushing her fingers up *underneath* the hair on her head, and the hair, *the entire head of hair,* lifted upwards all in one piece, and the hand slid underneath the hair and went on scratching!

She was wearing a wig! She was also wearing gloves! I glanced swiftly around at the rest of the now seated audience. *Every one of them was wearing gloves!*

My blood turned to ice. I began to shake all over. I glanced frantically behind me for a back door to escape through. There wasn't one.

Should I leap out from behind the screen and make a dash for the double-doors?

Those double-doors were already closed and I could see a woman standing in front of them. She was bending forward and fixing some sort of a metal chain round the two door-handles.

Keep still, I told myself. No one has seen you yet. There's no reason in the world why they should come and look behind the screen. But one false move, one cough, one sneeze, one nose-blow, one little sound of any sort and it won't be just one witch that gets

you. It'll be two hundred!

At that point, I think I fainted. The whole thing was altogether too much for a small boy to cope with. But I don't believe I was out for more than a few seconds, and when I came to, I was lying on the carpet and I was still, thank heavens, behind the screen. There was absolute silence all around me.

Rather shakily, I got to my knees and peered once again through the crack in the screen.

Chapter Seven

FRIZZLED LIKE A FRITTER

All the women, or rather the witches, were now sitting motionless in their chairs and staring as though hypnotized at somebody who had suddenly appeared on the platform. That somebody was another woman.

The first thing I noticed about this woman was her size. She was tiny, probably no more than four and a half feet tall. She looked quite young, I guessed about twenty-five or six, and she was very pretty. She had on a rather stylish long black dress that reached right to the ground and she wore black gloves that came up to her elbows. Unlike the others, she wasn't wearing a hat.

She didn't look to me like a witch at all, but she couldn't possibly *not* be one, otherwise what on earth was she doing up there on the platform? And why, for heaven's sake, were all the other witches gazing at her with such a mixture of adoration, awe and fear?

Very slowly, the young lady on the platform raised her hands to her face. I saw her gloved fingers unhooking something behind her ears, and then . . . then she caught hold of her cheeks and lifted her face clean away! The whole of that pretty face came away in her hands!

It was a mask!

As she took off the mask, she turned sideways and placed it carefully upon a small table nearby, and when she turned round again and faced us, I very nearly screamed out loud.

That face of hers was the most frightful and frightening thing I have ever seen. Just looking at it gave me the shakes all over. It was so crumpled and wizened, so shrunken and shrivelled, it looked as though it had been pickled in vinegar. It was a fearsome and ghastly sight. There was something terribly wrong with it, something foul and putrid and decayed. It seemed quite literally to be rotting away at the edges, and in the middle of the face, around the mouth and cheeks, I could see the skin all cankered and worm-eaten, as though maggots were working away in there.

There are times when something is so frightful you become mesmerized by it and can't look away. I was like that now. I was transfixed. I was numbed. I was magnetized by the sheer horror of this woman's features. But there was more to it than that. There was a look of serpents in those eyes of hers as they flashed around the audience.

I knew immediately, of course, that this was none other than The Grand High Witch herself. I knew also why she had worn a mask. She could never have moved around in public, let alone book in at a hotel, with her real face. Everyone who saw her would have run away screaming.

'The doors!' shouted The Grand High Witch in a voice that filled the room and bounced around the walls. 'Are they chained and bolted?'

'The doors are chained and bolted, Your Grandness,' answered a voice in the audience.

The brilliant snake's eyes that were set so deep in that dreadful rotting worm-eaten face glared unblinkingly at the witches who sat

facing her. 'You may rrree-moof your gloves!' she shouted.

Her voice, I noticed, had that same hard metallic quality as the voice of the witch I had met under the conker tree, only it was far louder and much much harsher. It rasped. It grated. It snarled. It scraped. It shrieked. And it growled.

Everyone in the room was peeling off her gloves. I was watching the hands of those in the back row. I wanted very much to see what their fingers looked like and whether my grandmother had been right. Ah! . . . Yes! . . . I could see several of them now! I could see the brown claws curving over the tips of the fingers! They were about two inches long, those claws, and sharp at the ends!

'You may rrree-moof your shoes!' barked The Grand High Witch. I heard a sigh of relief going up from all the witches in the room as they kicked off their narrow high-heeled shoes, and then I got a glimpse under the chairs of several pairs of stockinged feet, square and completely toeless. Revolting they were, as though the toes had been sliced away from the feet with a carving-knife.

'You may rrree-moof your vigs!' snarled The Grand High Witch. She had a peculiar way of speaking. There was some sort of a foreign accent there, something harsh and guttural, and she seemed to have trouble pronouncing the letter w. As well as that, she did something funny with the letter r. She would roll it round and round her mouth like a piece of hot pork-crackling before spitting it out. 'Rrree-moof your vigs and get some fresh air into your spotty scalps!' she shouted, and another sigh of relief arose from the audience as all the hands went up to the heads and all the wigs (with the hats still on them) were lifted away.

There now appeared in front of me row upon row of bald female heads, a sea of naked scalps, every one of them red and itchy-looking from being rubbed by the linings of the wigs. I simply cannot tell you how awful they were, and somehow the whole sight was made more grotesque because underneath those frightful scabby bald heads, the bodies were dressed in fashionable and rather pretty clothes. It was monstrous. It was unnatural.

Oh, heavens, I thought. Oh, help! Oh, Lord have mercy on me! These foul bald-headed females are child-killers every one of them, and here I am imprisoned in the same room and I can't escape!

At that point, a new and doubly horrifying thought struck me. My grandmother had said that with their special nose-holes they could smell out a child on a pitch-black night from right across the other side of the road. Up to now, my grandmother had been right every time. It seemed a certainty therefore that one of the witches in the back row was going to sniff me out at any moment and then the yell of 'Dogs' droppings!' would go up all over the room and I would be cornered like a rat.

I knelt on the carpet behind the screen, hardly daring to breathe.

Then suddenly I remembered another very important thing my grandmother had told me. 'The dirtier you are,' she had said, 'the harder it is for a witch to smell you out.'

How long since I had last had a bath?

Not for ages. I had my own room in the hotel and my grandmother never bothered with silly things like that. Come to think of it, I don't believe I'd had a bath since we arrived.

When had I last washed my hands or face?

Certainly not this morning.

Not yesterday either.

I glanced down at my hands. They were covered with smudge and mud and goodness knows what else besides.

So perhaps I had a chance after all. The stink-waves couldn't possibly get out through all that dirt.

'Vitches of Inkland!' shouted The Grand High Witch. She herself I noticed had not taken off either her wig or her gloves or her shoes. 'Vitches of Inkland!' she yelled.

The audience stirred uneasily and sat up straighter in their chairs.

'Miserrrable vitches!' she yelled. 'Useless lazy vitches! Feeble frrribbling vitches! You are a heap of idle good-for-nothing vurms!'

A shudder went through the audience. The Grand High Witch was clearly in an ugly mood and they knew it. I had a feeling that something awful was going to happen soon.

'I am having my breakfast this morning,' cried The Grand High Witch, 'and I am looking out of the vindow at the beach, and vot am I seeing? I am asking you, *vot am I seeing?* I am seeing a rrreevolting sight! I am seeing hundreds, I am seeing *thousands* of rrrotten rrreepulsive little children playing on the sand! It is putting me rrright off my food! *Vye have you not got rrrid of them?*' she screamed. 'Vye have you not rrrubbed them all out, these filthy smelly children?'

With each word she spoke, flecks of pale-blue phlegm shot from her mouth like little bullets.

'I am asking you *vye!*' she screamed.

Nobody answered her question.

'Children smell!' she screamed. 'They stink out the vurld! Vee do not vont these children around here!'

The bald heads in the audience all nodded vigorously.

'Vun child a veek is no good to me!' The Grand High Witch cried out. 'Is that the best you can do?'

'We will do better,' murmured the audience. 'We will do much better.'

'Better is no good either!' shrieked The Grand High Witch. 'I demand maximum rrree-sults! So here are my orders! My orders are that every single child in this country shall be rrrubbed out, sqvashed, sqvirted, sqvittered and frrrittered before I come here again in vun year's time! Do I make myself clear?'

A great gasp went up from the audience. I saw the witches all looking at one another with deeply troubled expressions. And I heard one witch at the end of the front row saying aloud, '*All* of them! We can't possibly wipe out *all* of them!'

The Grand High Witch whipped round as though someone had stuck a skewer into her bottom. 'Who said that?' she snapped. 'Who dares to argue vith me? It vos you, vos it not?' She pointed a gloved finger as sharp as a needle at the witch who had spoken.

'I didn't mean it, Your Grandness!' the witch cried out. 'I didn't mean to argue! I was just talking to myself!'

'You dared to argue vith me!' screamed The Grand High Witch.

'I was just talking to myself!' cried the wretched witch. 'I swear it, Your Grandness!' She began to shake with fear.

The Grand High Witch took a quick step forward, and when she spoke again, it was in a voice that made my blood run cold.

'A stupid vitch who answers back
Must burn until her bones are black!'

she screamed.

'No, no!' begged the witch in the front row. The Grand High Witch went on,

'A foolish vitch vithout a brain
Must sizzle in the fiery flame!'

'Save me!' cried the wretched witch in the front row. The Grand High Witch took no notice of her. She spoke again.

'An idiotic vitch like you
Must rrroast upon the barbecue!'

'Forgive me, O Your Grandness!' cried the miserable culprit. 'I didn't mean it!' But The Grand High Witch continued with her terrible recital.

'A vitch who dares to say I'm wrrrong
Vill not be vith us very long!'

A moment later, a stream of sparks that looked like tiny white-hot metal-filings came shooting out of The Grand High Witch's eyes and flew straight towards the one who had dared to speak. I saw the sparks striking against her and burrowing into her and she screamed a horrible howling scream and a puff of smoke rose up around her. A smell of burning meat filled the room.

Nobody moved. Like me, they were all watching the smoke, and when it had cleared away, the chair was empty. I caught a glimpse of something wispy-white, like a little cloud, fluttering upwards and disappearing out of the window.

A great sigh rose up from the audience.

The Grand High Witch glared around the room. 'I hope nobody else is going to make me cross today,' she remarked.

There was a deathly silence.

'Frrrizzled like a frrritter,' said The Grand High Witch. 'Cooked like a carrot. You vill never see *her* again. Now vee can get down to business.'

Chapter Eight

FORMULA 86 DELAYED ACTION MOUSE-MAKER

'Children are rrree-volting!' screamed The Grand High Witch. 'Vee vill vipe them all avay! Vee vill scrrrub them off the face of the earth! Vee vill flush them down the drain!'

'Yes, yes!' chanted the audience. 'Wipe them away! Scrub them off the earth! Flush them down the drain!'

'Children are foul and filthy!' thundered The Grand High Witch.

'They are! They are!' chorused the English witches. 'They are foul and filthy!'

'Children are dirty and stinky!' screamed The Grand High Witch.

'Dirty and stinky!' cried the audience, getting more and more worked up.

'Children are smelling of *dogs' drrroppings*!' screeched The Grand High Witch.

'Pooooooo!' cried the audience. 'Pooooooo! Pooooooo! Pooooooo!'

'They are vurse than dogs' drrroppings!' screeched The Grand High Witch. 'Dogs' drrroppings is smelling like violets and prrrimroses compared vith children!'

'Violets and primroses!' chanted the audience. They were clapping and cheering almost every word spoken from the platform. The speaker seemed to have them completely under her spell.

'To talk about children is making me sick!' screamed The Grand High Witch. 'I am feeling sick even *thinking* about them! Fetch me a basin!'

The Grand High Witch paused and glared at the mass of eager faces in the audience. They waited, wanting more.

'So now!' barked The Grand High Witch. 'So now I am having a plan! I am having a giganticus plan for getting rrrid of every single child in the whole of Inkland!'

The witches gasped. They gaped. They turned and gave each other ghoulish grins of excitement.

'Yes!' thundered The Grand High Witch. 'Vee shall svish them and svollop them and vee shall make to disappear every single smelly little brrrat in Inkland in vun strrroke!'

'Whoopee!' cried the witches, clapping their hands. 'You are brilliant, O Your Grandness! You are fantabulous!'

'Shut up and listen!' snapped The Grand High Witch. 'Listen very carefully and let us not be having any muck-ups!'

The audience leaned forward, eager to learn how this magic was going to be performed.

'Each and every vun of you,' thundered The Grand High Witch, 'is to go back to your home towns immediately and rrree-sign from your jobs. Rrree-sign! Give notice! Rrree-tire!'

'We will!' they cried. 'We will resign from our jobs!'

'And after you have rrree-signed from your jobs,' The Grand High Witch went on, 'each and every vun of you vill be going out and you vill be buying . . .' She paused.

'What will we be buying?' they cried. 'Tell us, O Brilliant One, what is it we shall be buying?'

'Sveet-shops!' shouted The Grand High Witch.

'Sweet-shops!' they cried. 'We are going to buy sweet-shops! What a frumptious wheeze!'

'Each of you vill be buying for herself a sveet-shop. You vill be buying the very best and most rrree-spectable sveet-shops in Inkland.'

'We will! We will!' they answered. Their dreadful voices were like a chorus of dentists' drills all grinding away together.

'I am vonting no tuppenny-ha'penny crrrummy little tobacco-selling-newspaper-sveet-shops!' shouted The Grand High Witch. 'I am vonting you to get only the very best shops filled up high vith piles and piles of luscious sveets and tasty chocs!'

'The best!' they cried. 'We shall buy the best sweet-shops in town!'

'You vill be having no trouble in getting vot you vont,' shouted The Grand High Witch, 'because you vill be offering four times as much as a shop is vurth and nobody is rrree-fusing an offer like that! Money is not a prrroblem to us vitches as you know very vell. I have brrrought vith me six trrrunks stuffed full of Inklish banknotes, all new and crrrisp. And all of them,' she added with a fiendish leer, 'all of them home-made.'

The witches in the audience grinned, appreciating this joke.

At that point, one foolish witch got so excited at the possibilities presented by owning a sweet-shop that she leapt to her feet and shouted, 'The children will come flocking to my shop and I will feed them poisoned sweets and poisoned chocs and wipe them all out like weasels!'

The room became suddenly silent. I saw the tiny body of The Grand High Witch stiffen and then go rigid with rage. 'Who spoke?' she shrieked. 'It vos *you*! You over there!'

The culprit sat down fast and covered her face with her clawed hands.

'You blithering bumpkin!' screeched The Grand High Witch. 'You brrrainless bogvumper! Are you not rrree-alizing that if you are going rrround poisoning little children you vill be caught in five minutes flat? Never in my life am I hearing such a boshvolloping suggestion coming from a vitch!'

The entire audience cowered and shook. I'm quite sure they all thought, as I did, that the terrible white-hot sparks were about to start flying again.

Curiously enough, they didn't.

'If such a tomfiddling idea is all you can be coming up vith,' thundered The Grand High Witch, 'then it is no vunder Inkland is still svorming vith rrrotten little children!'

There was another silence. The Grand High Witch glared at the witches in the audience. 'Do you not know,' she shouted at them, 'that vee vitches are vurrrking only vith magic?'

'We know, Your Grandness!' they all answered. 'Of course we know!'

The Grand High Witch grated her bony gloved hands against each other and cried out, 'So each of you is owning a magnificent sveet-shop! The next move is that each of you vill be announcing in the vindow of your shop that on a certain day you vill be having a Great Gala Opening vith frree sveets and chocs to every child!'

'That will bring them in, the greedy little brutes!' cried the audience. 'They'll be fighting to get through the doors!'

'Next,' continued The Grand High Witch, 'you vill prepare yourselves for this Great Gala Opening by filling every choc and every sveet in your shop vith my very latest and grrreatest magic formula! This is known as FORMULA 86 DELAYED ACTION MOUSE-MAKER!'

'Delayed Action Mouse-Maker!' they chanted. 'She's done it again! Her Grandness has concocted yet another of her wondrous magic child-killers! How do we make it, O Brilliant One?'

'Exercise patience,' answered The Grand High Witch. 'First, I am explaining to you how my Formula 86 Delayed Action Mouse-Maker is vurrrking. Listen carefully.'

'We are listening!' cried the audience who were now jumping up and down in their chairs with excitement.

'Delayed Action Mouse-Maker is a green liqvid,' explained The Grand High Witch, 'and vun droplet in each choc or sveet vill be qvite enough. So here is vot happens:

'Child eats choc vich has in it Delayed Action Mouse-Maker liqvid . . .

'Child goes home feeling fine . . .

'Child goes to bed, still feeling fine . . .

'Child vakes up in the morning still OK . . .

'Child goes to school still feeling fine . . .

'Formula, you understand, is *delayed action*, and is not vurrrking yet.'

'We understand, O Brainy One!' cried the audience. 'But when does it start working?'

'It is starting to vurrrk at exactly nine o'clock, vhen the child is arriving at school!' shouted The Grand High Witch triumphantly. 'Child arrives at school. Delayed Action Mouse-Maker immediately starts to vurrrk. Child starts to shrrrink. Child is starting to grow fur. Child is starting to grow tail. All is happening in prrreecisely twenty-six seconds. After twenty-six seconds, child is not a child any longer. It is a mouse!'

'A mouse!' cried the witches. 'What a frumptious thought!'

'Classrooms vill all be svorrming vith mice!' shouted The Grand High Witch. 'Chaos and pandemonium vill be rrreigning in every school in Inkland! Teachers vill be hopping up and down! Vimmen teachers vill be standing on desks and holding up skirts and yelling, "Help, help, help!"'

'They will! They will!' cried the audience.

'And vot,' shouted The Grand High Witch, 'is happening next in every school?'

'Tell us!' they cried. 'Tell us, O Brainy One!'

The Grand High Witch stretched her stringy neck forward and grinned at the audience, showing two rows of pointed teeth, slightly blue. She raised her voice louder than ever and shouted, *'Mouse-trrraps is coming out!'*

'Mouse-traps!' cried the witches.

'And cheese!' shouted The Grand High Witch. 'Teachers is all rrrushing and rrrunning out and getting mouse-trrraps and baiting them vith cheese and putting them down all over school! Mice is nibbling cheese! Mouse-trrraps is going off! All over school, mouse-trrraps is going *snappety-snap* and mouse-heads is rrrolling across the floors like marbles! All over Inkland, in everrry school in Inkland, noise of snapping mouse-trrraps vill be heard!'

At this point, the disgusting old Grand High Witch began to do a sort of witch's dance up and down the platform, stamping her feet and clapping her hands. The entire audience joined in the clapping and the foot-stamping. They were making such a tremendous racket that I thought surely Mr Stringer would hear it and come banging at the door. But he didn't.

Then, above all the noise, I heard the voice of The Grand High Witch screaming out some sort of an awful gloating song,

'Down vith children! Do them in!
Boil their bones and fry their skin!
Bish them, sqvish them, bash them, mash them!
Brrreak them, shake them, slash them, smash them!
Offer chocs vith magic powder!
Say "Eat up!" then say it louder.
Crrram them full of sticky eats,
Send them home still guzzling sveets.
And in the morning little fools

Go marching off to separate schools.
A girl feels sick and goes all pale.
She yells, "Hey look! I've grrrown a tail!"
A boy who's standing next to her
Screams, "Help! I think I'm grrrowing fur!"
Another shouts, "Vee look like frrreaks!
There's viskers growing on our cheeks!"
A boy who vos extremely tall
Cries out, "Vot's wrong? I'm grrrowing small!"
Four tiny legs begin to sprrrout
From everybody rrround about.
And all at vunce, all in a trrrice,
There are no children! Only MICE!
In every school is mice galore
All rrrunning rrround the school-rrroom floor!
And all the poor demented teachers
Is yelling, "Hey, who are these crrreatures?"
They stand upon the desks and shout,
"Get out, you filthy mice! Get out!
Vill someone fetch some mouse-trrraps, please!
And don't forrrget to bring the cheese!"
Now mouse-trrraps come and every trrrap
Goes *snippy-snip* and *snappy-snap*.
The mouse-trrraps have a powerful spring,
The springs go *crack* and *snap* and *ping*!
Is lovely noise for us to hear!
Is music to a vitch's ear!
Dead mice is every place arrround,

Piled two feet deep upon the grrround,
Vith teachers searching left and rrright,
But not a single child in sight!
The teachers cry, "Vot's going on?
Oh vhere have all the children gone?
Is half-past nine and as a rrrule
They're never late as this for school!"
Poor teachers don't know vot to do.
Some sit and rrread, and just a few
Amuse themselves throughout the day
By sveeping all the mice avay.
AND ALL US VITCHES SHOUT HOORAY!

Chapter Nine

THE RECIPE

I hope you haven't forgotten that while all this was going on I was still stuck behind the screen on my hands and knees with one eye glued to the crack. I don't know how long I had been there but it seemed like for ever. The worst part of it was not being allowed to cough or make a sound, and knowing that if I did, I was as good as dead. And all the way through, I was living in constant terror that one of the witches in the back row was going to get a whiff of my presence through those special nose-holes of hers.

My only hope, as I saw it, was the fact that I hadn't washed for days. That and the never-ending excitement and clapping and shouting that was going on in the room. The witches were thinking of nothing except The Grand High Witch up there on the platform and her great plan for wiping out all the children of England. They certainly weren't sniffing around for a child in the room. In their wildest dreams (if witches have dreams), that would never have occurred to any of them. I kept still and prayed.

The Grand High Witch's dreadful gloating song was over now, and the audience was clapping madly and shouting, 'Brilliant! Sensational! Marvellous! You are a genius, O Brainy One! It is a thrilling invention, this Delayed Action Mouse-Maker! It is a winner! And the beauty of it is that the teachers will be the ones who bump off the stinking little children! It won't be us doing it! We shall never be caught!'

'Vitches are never caught!' snapped The Grand High Witch. 'Attention now! I vont everybody's attention for I am about to be telling you vot you must do to prepare Formula 86 Delayed Action Mouse-Maker!'

Suddenly there came a great gasp from the audience. This was followed by a hubbub of shrieking and yelling, and I saw many of the witches leaping to their feet and pointing at the platform and crying out, 'Mice! Mice! Mice! She's done it to show us! The Brainy One has turned two children into mice and there they are!'

I looked towards the platform. The mice were there all right, two of them, running around near The Grand High Witch's skirts.

But these were not field mice or house mice or wood mice or harvest mice. They were *white mice*! I recognized them immediately as being my own little William and Mary!

'Mice!' shouted the audience. 'Our leader has made mice to appear out of nowhere! Get the mouse-traps! Fetch the cheese!'

I saw The Grand High Witch peering down at the floor and staring with obvious puzzlement at William and Mary. She bent lower to get a closer look. Then she straightened up and shouted, 'Qviet!'

The audience became silent and sat down.

'These mice are nothing to do vith me!' she shouted. 'These mice are *pet* mice! These mice are qvite obviously belonging to some rrreepellent little child in the hotel! A boy it vill be for a certainty because girls are not keeping pet mice!'

'A boy!' cried the witches. 'A filthy smelly little boy! We'll swipe him! We'll swizzle him! We'll have his tripes for breakfast!'

'Silence!' shouted The Grand High Witch, raising her hands. 'You know perrrfectly vell you must do nothing to drrraw attention to yourselves vhile you are living in the hotel! Let us by all means get rrrid of this evil-smelling little sqvirt, but vee must do it as qvietly as possible, for are vee not all of us the most rrree-spectable ladies of the Rrroyal Society for the Prrree-vention of Crrruelty to Children?'

'What do you suggest then, O Brainy One?' they cried out. 'How shall we dispose of this small pile of filth?'

They're talking about me, I thought. These females are actually talking about how to kill me. I began to sweat.

'Whoever he is, he is not important,' announced The Grand High Witch. 'Leave him to me. I shall smell him out and turn him into a mackerel and have him dished up for supper.'

'Bravo!' cried the witches. 'Cut off his head and chop off his tail and fry him in hot butter!'

You can imagine that none of this was making me feel very comfortable. William and Mary were still running around on the platform, and I saw The Grand High Witch aim a swift running

kick at William. She caught him right on the point of her toe and sent him flying. She did the same to Mary. Her aim was extraordinary. She would have made a great football player. Both mice crashed against the wall, and for a few moments they lay stunned. Then they got to their feet and scampered away.

'Attention again!' The Grand High Witch was shouting. 'I vill now give to you the rrrecipe for concocting Formula 86 Delayed Action Mouse-Maker! Get out pencils and paper.'

Handbags were opened all over the room and notebooks were fished out.

'Give us the recipe, O Brainy One!' cried the audience impatiently. 'Tell us the secret.'

'First,' said The Grand High Witch, 'I had to find something that vould cause the children to become very small very qvickly.'

'And what was that?' cried the audience.

'That part vos simple,' said The Grand High Witch. 'All you have to do if you are vishing to make a child very small is to look at him through the wrrrong end of a telescope.'

'She's a wonder!' cried the audience. 'Who else would have thought of a thing like that?'

'So you take the wrrrong end of a telescope,' continued The Grand High Witch, 'and you boil it until it gets soft.'

'How long does that take?' they asked her.

'Tventy-vun hours of boiling,' answered The Grand High Witch. 'And vhile this is going on, you take exactly forty-five brrrown mice and you chop off their tails vith a carving-knife and you fry the tails in hair-oil until they are nice and crrrisp.'

'What do we do with all those mice who have had their tails chopped off?' asked the audience.

'You simmer them in frog-juice for vun hour,' came the answer. 'But listen to me. So far I have only given you the easy part of the rrrecipe. The rrreally difficult problem is to put in something that vill have a genuine delayed action rrree-sult, something that can be eaten by children on a certain day but vhich vill not start vurrrking on them until

nine o'clock the next morning vhen they arrive at school.'

'What did you come up with, O Brainy One?' they called out. 'Tell us the great secret!'

'The secret,' announced The Grand High Witch triumphantly, 'is an *alarm-clock*!'

'An alarm-clock!' they cried. 'It's a stroke of genius!'

'Of course it is,' said The Grand High Witch. 'You can set a tventy-four-hour alarm-clock today and at exactly nine o'clock tomorrow it vill go off.'

'But we will need five million alarm-clocks!' cried the audience. 'We will need one for each child!'

'Idiots!' shouted The Grand High Witch. 'If you are vonting a steak, you do not cook the whole cow! It is the same vith alarm-clocks. Vun clock vill make enough for a thousand children. Here is vhat you do. You set your alarm-clock to go off at nine o'clock tomorrow morning. Then you rrroast it in the oven until it is crrrisp and tender. Are you wrrriting this down?'

'We are, Your Grandness, we are!' they cried.

'Next,' said The Grand High Witch, 'you take your boiled

telescope and your frrried mouse-tails and your cooked mice and your rrroasted alarm-clock and all together you put them into the mixer. Then you mix them at full speed. This vill give you a nice thick paste. Vhile the mixer is still mixing you must add to it the yolk of vun grrruntle's egg.'

76

'A gruntle's egg!' cried the audience. 'We shall do that!'

Underneath all the clamour that was going on I heard one witch in the back row saying to her neighbour, 'I'm getting a bit old to go bird's nesting. Those ruddy gruntles always nest very high up.'

'So you mix in the egg,' The Grand High Witch went on, 'and vun after the other you also mix in the following items: the claw of a crrrabcrrruncher, the beak

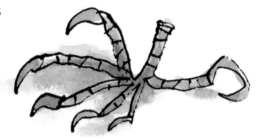

of a blabbersnitch, the snout of a grrrobblesqvirt and the tongue of a catsprrringer. I trust you are not having any trrrouble finding those.'

'None at all!' they cried out. 'We will spear the blabbersnitch and trap the crabcruncher and shoot the grobblesquirt and catch the catspringer in his burrow!'

'Excellent!' said The Grand High Witch. 'Vhen you have mixed everything together in the mixer, you vill have a

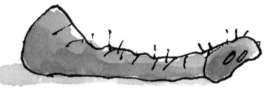

most marvellous-looking grrreen liqvid. Put vun drop, just vun titchy droplet, of this liqvid into a chocolate or a sveet, and *at nine o'clock the next morning* the child who ate it vill turn into a mouse in

tventy-six seconds! But vun vurd of vorning. Never increase the dose. Never put more than vun drrrop into each sveet or chocolate.

And never give more than vun sweet or chocolate to each child. An overdose of Delayed Action Mouse-Maker vill mess up the timing of the alarm-clock and cause the child to turn into a mouse too early. A large overdose might even have an instant effect, and you vouldn't vont that, vould you? You vouldn't vont the children turning into mice rrright there in your sveet-shops. That vould give the game away. So be very carrreful! Do not overdose!'

Chapter Ten

Bruno Jenkins Disappears

The Grand High Witch was starting to talk again. 'I am now going to prrrove to you,' she said, 'that this rrrecipe is vurrrking to perrrfection. You understand, of course, that you can set the alarm-clock to go off at any time you like. It does not *have* to be nine o'clock. So yesterday I am personally prrree-paring a small qvantity of the magic formula in order to give to you a public demonstration. But I am making vun small change in the rrrecipe. Before I am rrroasting the alarm-clock, I am setting it to go off, not at nine o'clock the next morning, but at half-past thrrree the next afternoon. Vhich means half-past thrrree *this* afternoon. And that,' she said, glancing at her wrist-watch, 'is in prrree-cisely seven minutes' time!'

The audience of witches was listening intently, sensing that something dramatic was about to happen.

'So vot am I doing yesterday vith this magic liqvid?' asked The Grand High Witch. 'I vill tell you vot I am doing. I am putting vun drrroplet of it into a very sqvishy chocolate bar and I am giving this bar to a rrree-pulsive smelly little boy who is hanging rrround the lobby of the hotel.'

The Grand High Witch paused. The audience remained silent, waiting for her to go on.

'I votched this rrree-pulsive little brrrute gobbling up the sqvishy bar of chocolate and vhen he had finished, I said to him, "Vos that good?" He said it vos great. So I said to him, "Vould you like some

79

more?" And he said, "Yes." So I said, "I vill give you *six* more chocolate bars like that if you vill meet me in the Ballroom of this hotel at twenty-five-past thrrree tomorrow afternoon." "Six bars!" cried this greedy little svine. "I'll be there! You bet I'll be there!"

'So the stage is set!' shouted The Grand High Witch. 'The prrroof of the pudding is about to begin! Do not forget that before I am rrroasting the alarm-clock yesterday, I am setting it for half-past thrrree today. It is now' – she glanced again at her watch – 'it is now exactly twenty-five minutes past thrrree and the nasty little stinker who vill be turning into a mouse in five minutes' time should at this very moment be standing outside the doors!'

And by gum, she was absolutely right. The boy, whoever he might be, was already rattling the door-handle and banging on the doors with his fist.

'Qvick!' shrieked The Grand High Witch. 'Put on your vigs! Put on your gloves! Put on your shoes!'

There was a great rustle and bustle of putting on wigs and gloves and shoes, and I saw The Grand High Witch herself reach for her face-mask and put it on over that revolting face of hers. It was astonishing how that mask transformed her. All of a sudden she became once again a rather pretty young lady.

'Let me in!' came the boy's voice from behind the doors. 'Where are those chocolate bars you promised me? I'm here to collect! Dish them out!'

'He is not only smelly, he is also grrreedy,' said The Grand High Witch. 'Rrree-moof the chains from the doors and let him come in.' The extraordinary thing about the mask was that its lips moved quite naturally when she spoke. You really couldn't see it was a mask at all.

One of the witches leapt to her feet and unfastened the chains.

She opened the two huge doors. Then I heard her saying, 'Why *hello*, little man. How lovely to see you. You have come for your chocolate bars, have you not? They are all ready for you. Do come in.'

A small boy wearing a white T-shirt and grey shorts and gymshoes entered the room. I recognized him at once. He was called Bruno Jenkins and he was staying in the hotel with his parents. I didn't care for him. He was one of those boys who is always eating something whenever you meet him. Meet him in the hotel lobby and he is stuffing sponge cake into his mouth. Pass him in the corridor and he is fishing potato crisps out of a bag by the fistful. Catch sight of him in the hotel garden and he is wolfing a Dairy Milk Bar and has two more sticking out of his trouser-pocket. What's more, Bruno never stopped boasting about how his father made more money than my father and that they owned three cars. But worse than that, yesterday morning I had found him kneeling on the flagstones of the hotel terrace with a magnifying-glass in his hand. There was a column of ants marching across one of the flagstones and Bruno Jenkins was focusing the sun through his magnifying-glass and roasting the ants one by one. 'I like watching them burn,' he said. 'That's horrible!' I cried. 'Stop doing it!' 'Let's see you stop me,' he said. At that point I had pushed him with all my might and he had crashed sideways on to the flagstones. His magnifying-glass had splintered into many pieces and he had leapt up shrieking, 'My father is going to get you for this!' Then he had run off, presumably to find his wealthy dad. That was the last time I had seen Bruno Jenkins until now. I doubted very much that he was about to be turned into a mouse, although I must confess that I was secretly hoping it might happen. Either way, I didn't envy him being up there in front of all those witches.

'Darling boy,' cooed The Grand High Witch from up on the

platform. 'I have your chocolates all rrready for you. Do come up here firrrst and say hello to all these lovely ladies.' Her voice was quite different now. It was soft and gentle and absolutely dripping with syrup.

Bruno was looking a bit bewildered, but he allowed himself to be led up on to the platform, where he stood beside The Grand High Witch and said, 'OK, where are my six bars of chocolate?'

I saw the witch who had let him in quietly putting the chain back on the door-handles. Bruno didn't notice this. He was too busy asking for his chocolate.

'The time is now vun minute before half-past thrrree!' announced The Grand High Witch.

'What the heck's going on?' Bruno asked. He wasn't frightened, but he wasn't looking exactly comfortable either. 'What *is* this?' he said. 'Gimme my chocolate!'

'Thirty seconds to go!' cried The Grand High Witch, gripping Bruno by the arm. Bruno shook himself clear and stared at her. She stared back at him, smiling with the lips of her mask. Every witch in the audience was staring at Bruno.

'Tventy seconds!' cried The Grand High Witch.

'Gimme the chocolate!' shouted Bruno, becoming suddenly suspicious. 'Gimme the chocolate and let me out of here!'

'Fifteen seconds!' cried The Grand High Witch.

'Will one of you crazy punks kindly tell me what all this is about?' shouted Bruno.

'Ten seconds!' cried The Grand High Witch. 'Nine . . . eight . . . seven . . . six . . . five . . . four . . . thrrree . . . two . . . vun . . . zero! Vee have ignition!'

I could have sworn I heard an alarm-clock ringing. I saw Bruno jump. He jumped as though someone had stuck a hatpin deep into his bottom and he yelled, 'Ow!' He jumped so high that he landed on a small table up there on the stage, and he started hopping about on the top of this table, waving his arms and yelling his head off. Then suddenly he became silent. His whole body stiffened.

'The alarm has gone off!' shrieked The Grand High Witch. 'The Mouse-Maker is beginning to vurrrk!' She started hopping about

on the platform and clapping her gloved hands together and then
she shouted out,

> 'This smelly brrrat, this filthy scum
> This horrid little louse
> Vill very very soon become
> A lovely little MOUSE!'

Bruno was getting smaller by the second. I could see him
shrinking . . .

Now his clothes seemed to be disappearing and brown fur was
growing all over his body . . .

Suddenly he had a tail . . .

And then he had whiskers . . .

Now he had four feet . . .

It was all happening so quickly . . .

It was a matter of seconds only . . .

And all at once he wasn't there any more . . .

A small brown mouse was running around on the table top . . .

'Bravo!' yelled the audience. 'She's done it! It works! It's fantastic!
It's colossal! It's the greatest yet! You are a miracle, O Brainy One!'
They were all standing up and clapping and cheering and

The Grand High Witch produced a mouse-trap from the folds of her dress and started to set it.

Oh no! I thought. I don't want to see this! Bruno Jenkins may have been a bit of a stinker but I'm dashed if I want to watch him having his head chopped off!

'Vhere is he?' snapped The Grand High Witch, searching the platform. 'Vhere has that mouse got to?'

She couldn't find him. Clever Bruno must have jumped down off the table and scampered off into some corner or even down a small hole. Thank heavens for that.

'It matters not!' shouted The Grand High Witch. 'Silence and sit down!'

Chapter Eleven

The Ancient Ones

The Grand High Witch stood on the very centre of the platform, and those dangerous eyes of hers travelled slowly around the audience of witches who were sitting so meekly before her. 'All those over seventy put up your hands!' she barked suddenly.

Seven or eight hands went up in the air.

'It comes to me,' said The Grand High Witch, 'that you ancient vuns vill not be able to climb high trrrees in search of grrruntles' eggs.'

'We won't, Your Grandness! We are afraid we won't!' chanted the ancient ones.

'Nor vill you be able to catch the crrrabcrrruncher, who lives high up on rrrocky cliffs,' The Grand High Witch went on. 'I can't exactly see you sprrrinting after the speedy catsprrringer either, or diving into deep vorters to spear the blabbersnitch, or striding the bleak moors with a gun under your arm to shoot the grrrobblesqvirt. You are too old and feeble for those things.'

'We are,' chanted the ancient ones. 'We are! We are!'

'You ancient vuns have served me vell over many years,' said The Grand High Witch, 'and I do not vish to deny you the pleasure of bumping off a few thousand children each just because you have become old and feeble. I have therefore prepared personally vith my own hands a limited qvantity of Delayed Action Mouse-Maker vhich I vill distrrribute to the ancient vuns before you leave the hotel.'

'Oh, thank you, thank you!' cried the old witches. 'You are far too good to us, Your Grandness! You are so kind and thoughtful!'

'Here is a sample of vot I am giving you,' shouted The Grand High Witch. She fished around in a pocket of her dress and brought out a very small bottle. She held it up and shouted, 'In this tiny bottle is five hundred doses of Mouse-Maker! Is enough to turrrn five hundred children into mice!' I could see that the bottle was made of dark-blue glass and that it was very small, about the same size as the ones you can buy at the chemist with nose-drops in them. 'Each of you ancient vuns vill get two of these bottles!' she shouted.

'Thank you, thank you, O Most Generous and Thoughtful One!' chorused the ancient witches. 'Not one drop will be wasted! Each of us will promise to squish and squallop and squiggle one thousand children!'

'Our meeting is over!' announced The Grand High Witch. 'Here is the time-table for the rrreemainder of your stay in this hotel.

'Rrright now, vee must all go out on to the Sunshine Terrace and have tea vith that rrridiculous Manager.

'Next, at six o'clock tonight, those vitches who are too old to climb trees after grrruntles' eggs vill rrree-port to my rrroom to rrree-ceive two bottles each of Mouse-Maker. My rrroom number is 454. Do not forget it.

'Then, at eight o'clock, all of you vill assemble in the Dining-Rrroom for supper. Vee are the lovely ladies of the RSPCC and they are setting up two long tables specially for us. But do not forget to put the cotton plugs up your noses. That Dining-Rrroom vill be full of filthy little children and vithout the nose-plugs the stink vill be unbearrable. Apart from that, rrree-member to behave normally at all times. Is everything clear? Any qvestions?'

'I have one question, Your Grandness,' said a voice in the audience. 'What happens if one of the chocolates we are giving away in our shops gets eaten by a grown-up?'

'That's just too bad for the grrrown-up,' said The Grand High Witch. 'This meeting is over!' she shouted. 'Out you go!'

The witches stood up and began gathering their things together. I was watching them through the crack and hoping to heaven they would hurry up and leave so that I might be safe at last.

'*Wait!*' shrieked one of the witches in the back row. '*Hold everything!*' Her shrieking voice echoed through the Ballroom like a trumpet. All the witches suddenly stopped and turned and looked towards the speaker. She was one of the taller witches and I could see her standing there with her head tilted back and her nose in the air and she was sucking in great long breaths of air through those curvy pink sea-shelly nostrils of hers.

'*Wait!*' she shouted again.

'What is it?' the others cried out.

'Dogs' droppings!' she yelled. 'Just then I got a whiff of dogs' droppings!'

'Surely not!' the others shouted. 'There couldn't be!'

'Yes yes!' shouted the first witch. 'There it is again! It's not strong! But it's there! I mean it's here! It's definitely somewhere not too far away!'

'Vot's going on down there?' shouted The Grand High Witch, glaring down from the platform.

'Mildred's just got a whiff of dogs' droppings, Your Grandness!' someone called back to her.

'Vot rrrubbish is this?' shouted The Grand High Witch. 'She has dogs' drrroppings on the brain! There are no children in this rrrroom!'

'Hang on!' cried the witch called Mildred. 'Hang on, everybody! Don't move! I'm getting it again!' Her huge curvy nose-holes were waving in and out like a pair of fish-tails. 'It's getting stronger! It's hitting me harder now! Can't the rest of you smell it?'

All the noses of all the witches in that room went up in the air, and all the nostrils began to suck and sniff.

'She's right!' cried another voice. 'She's absolutely right! Dogs' droppings it is, strong and foul!'

In a matter of seconds, the entire assembly of witches had taken up the dreaded cry of dogs' droppings. 'Dogs' droppings!' they shouted. 'The room is full of it! Poo! Poo-oo-oo-oo-oo-oo-ooo!

Why did we not smell it before? It stinks like a sewer! Some little
swine must be hiding not so very far away from here!'

'Find it!' screamed The Grand High Witch. 'Trrrack it down!
Rrrootle it out! Follow your noses till you get it!'

The hairs on my head were standing up like the bristles of a nail-
brush and a cold sweat was breaking out all over me.

'Rrrootle it out, this small lump of dung!' screeched The Grand
High Witch. 'Don't let it escape! If it is in here it has observed the
most secret things! It must be exterrrminated immediately!'

Chapter Twelve

METAMORPHOSIS

I remember thinking to myself, *There is no escape for me now! Even if I make a run for it and manage to dodge the lot of them, I still won't get out because the doors are chained and locked! I'm finished! I'm done for! Oh, Grandmamma, what are they going to do to me?*

I looked round and I saw a hideous painted and powdered witch's face staring down at me, and the face opened its mouth and yelled triumphantly, 'It's here! It's behind the screen! Come and get it!' The witch reached out a gloved hand and grabbed me by the hair but I twisted free and jumped away. I ran, oh how I ran! The sheer terror of it all put wings on my feet! I flew around the outside of the great Ballroom and not one of them had a chance of catching me. As I came level with the doors, I paused and tried to open them but the big chain was on them and they didn't even rattle.

The witches were not bothering to chase me. They simply stood there in small groups, watching me and knowing for certain that there was no way I could escape. Several of them were holding their noses with gloved fingers and there were cries of, 'Poo! What a stink! We can't stand this much longer!'

'Catch it then, you idiots!' screamed The Grand High Witch from up on the platform. 'Sprrread out in a line across the room and close in on it and grab it! Corner this filthy little gumboil and seize it and bring it up here to me!'

The witches spread out as they were told. They advanced towards me, some from one end, some from the other, and some came down the middle between the rows of empty chairs. They were bound to get me now. They had me cornered.

From sheer and absolute terror, I began to scream. '*Help!*' I screamed, turning my head towards the doors in the hope that somebody outside might hear me. 'Help! Help! Hel-l-l-lp!'

'Get it!' shouted The Grand High Witch. 'Grrrab hold of it! Stop it yelling!'

They rushed at me then, and about five of them grabbed me by the arms and legs and lifted me clear off the ground. I went on screaming, but one of them clapped a gloved hand over my mouth and that stopped me.

'Brrring it here!' shouted The Grand High Witch. 'Brrring the spying little vurm up here to me!'

I was carried on to the platform with my arms and legs held tight by many hands, and I lay there suspended in the air, facing the ceiling. I saw The Grand High Witch standing over me, grinning at me in the most horrible way. She held up the small blue bottle of Mouse-Maker and she said, 'Now for a little medicine! Hold his nose to make him open his mouth!'

Strong fingers pinched my nose. I kept my mouth closed tight and held my breath. But I couldn't do it for long. My chest was bursting. I opened my mouth to get one big quick breath of air and as I did so, The Grand High Witch poured the entire contents of the little bottle down my throat!

Oh, the pain and the fire! It felt as though a kettleful of boiling water had been poured into my mouth. My throat was going up in flames! Then very quickly the frightful burning searing scorching feeling started spreading down into my chest and into my tummy and on and on into my arms and legs and all over my body! I screamed and screamed but once again the gloved hand was clapped over my lips. The next thing I felt was my skin beginning to tighten. How else can I describe it? It was quite literally a tightening and a shrinking of the skin all over my body from the top of my head to the tips of my fingers to the ends of my toes! I felt as though I was a balloon and somebody was twisting the top of the balloon and twisting and twisting and the balloon was getting smaller and smaller and the skin was getting tighter and tighter and soon it was going to burst.

Then the *squeezing* began. This time I was inside a suit of iron and somebody was turning a screw, and with each turn of the screw the iron suit became smaller and smaller so that I was squeezed like an orange into a pulpy mess with the juice running out of my sides.

After that there came a fierce prickling sensation all over my skin (or what was left of my skin) as though tiny needles were forcing their way out through the surface of the skin from the inside, and this, I realize now, was the growing of the mouse-fur.

Far away in the distance, I heard the voice of The Grand High Witch yelling, 'Five hundred doses! This stinking little carbuncle has had five hundred doses and the alarm-clock has been smashed and now vee are having *instantaneous action*!' I heard clapping and cheering and I remember thinking: *I am not myself any longer! I have gone clear out of my own skin!*

I noticed that the floor was only an inch from my nose.

I noticed also a pair of little furry front paws resting on the floor. I was able to move those paws. They were mine!

At that moment, I realized that I was not a little boy any longer. I was A MOUSE.

'Now for the mouse-trrrap!' I heard The Grand High Witch yelling. 'I've got it right here! And here's a piece of cheese!'

But I wasn't going to wait for that. I was off across the platform like a streak of lightning! I was astonished at my own speed! I leapt over witches' feet right and left, and in no time at all I was down

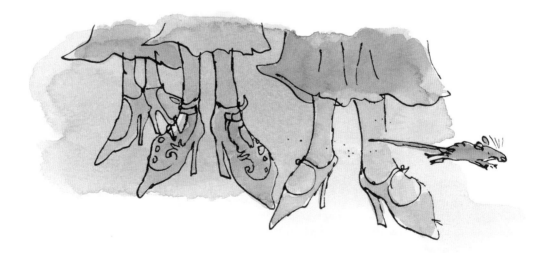

the steps and on to the floor of the Ballroom itself and skittering off among the rows of chairs. What I especially liked was the fact that I made no sound at all as I ran. I was a swift and silent mover. And quite amazingly, the pain had all gone now. I was feeling quite remarkably well. *It is not a bad thing after all*, I thought to myself, *to be tiny as well as speedy when there is a bunch of dangerous females after your blood*. I selected the back leg of a chair and squeezed up against it and kept very still.

In the distance, The Grand High Witch was shouting, 'Leave the little stinkpot alone! It is not vurth bothering about! It is only a mouse now! Somebody else vill soon catch it! Let us get out of here! The meeting is over! Unlock the doors and shove off to the Sunshine Terrace to have tea vith that idiotic Manager!'

Chapter Thirteen

BRUNO

$\mathcal{I}$ peeped round the leg of the chair and watched the hundreds of witches' feet walking out through the doors of the Ballroom. When they had all gone and the place was absolutely silent, I began to move cautiously about on the floor. Suddenly I remembered Bruno. He must surely be around here somewhere, too. 'Bruno!' I called out.

I wasn't seriously expecting that I would be able to speak at all now that I had become a mouse, so I got the shock of my life when I heard my own voice, my own perfectly normal rather loud voice, coming out of my tiny mouth.

It was wonderful. I was thrilled. I tried it again. 'Bruno Jenkins, where are you?' I called out. 'If you can hear me, give a shout!'

My voice was exactly the same and just as loud as it had been when I was a boy. 'Hey there, Bruno Jenkins!' I called. 'Where are you?'

There was no answer.

I pottered about between the seat-legs trying to get used to being so close to the ground. I decided I rather liked it. You are probably wondering why I wasn't depressed at all. I found myself thinking, *What's so wonderful about being a little boy anyway? Why is that necessarily any better than being a mouse? I know that mice get hunted and they sometimes get poisoned or caught in traps. But little boys sometimes get killed, too. Little boys can be run over by motor-cars or they can die of some awful illness. Little boys have to go to school. Mice don't. Mice don't have to pass exams. Mice don't have to worry about money. Mice, as far as I can see, have only two enemies, humans and cats. My grandmother is a human, but I know for certain that she will always love me whoever I am. And she never, thank goodness, keeps a cat. When mice grow up, they don't ever have to go to war and fight against other mice. Mice, I felt pretty certain, all like each other. People don't.*

Yes, I told myself, *I don't think it is at all a bad thing to be a mouse.*

I was wandering around the Ballroom floor thinking about all this when I spotted another mouse. It was crouching on the floor holding a piece of bread in its front paws and nibbling away at it with great gusto.

It had to be Bruno. 'Hello, Bruno,' I said.

He glanced up at me for about two seconds, then went right on guzzling.

'What have you found?' I asked him.

'One of them dropped it,' he answered. 'It's a fish-paste sandwich. Pretty good.'

He too spoke with a perfectly normal voice. One would have expected that a mouse (if it was going to talk at all) would do so with the smallest and squeakiest voice you could imagine. It was terrifically funny to hear the voice of the rather loud-mouthed Bruno coming out of that tiny mouse's throat.

'Listen, Bruno,' I said. 'Now that we are both mice, I think we ought to start thinking a bit about the future.'

He stopped eating and stared at me with small black eyes.

'What do you mean we?' he said. 'The fact that you're a mouse has nothing to do with me.'

'But you're a mouse, too, Bruno.'

'Don't be a fool,' he said. 'I'm not a mouse.'

'I'm afraid you are, Bruno.'

'I most certainly am not!' he shouted. 'Why are you insulting me? I haven't been rude to you! Why do you call *me* a mouse?'

'Don't you know what's happened to you?' I said.

'What on earth are you talking about?' Bruno said.

'I have to inform you,' I said, 'that not very long ago the witches turned you into a mouse. Then they did it to me.'

'You're lying!' he cried. 'I'm not a mouse!'

'If you hadn't been so busy guzzling that sandwich,' I said, 'you would have noticed your hairy paws. Take a look at them.'

Bruno looked down at his paws. He jumped. 'Good grief!' he cried. 'I *am* a mouse! You wait till my father hears about this!'

'He may think it's an improvement,' I said.

'I don't want to be a mouse!' Bruno shouted, jumping up and down. 'I refuse to be a mouse! I'm Bruno Jenkins!'

'There are worse things than being a mouse,' I said. 'You can live in a hole.'

'I don't want to live in a hole!' Bruno shouted.

'And you can creep into the larder at night,' I said, 'and nibble through all the packets of raisins and cornflakes and chocolate biscuits and everything else you can find. You can stay there all night eating yourself silly. That's what mice do.'

'Now that's a thought,' Bruno said, perking up a bit. 'But how am I going to open the door of the fridge to get at the cold chicken and all the leftovers? That's something I do every evening at home.'

'Maybe your rich father will get you a special little mouse-fridge all to yourself,' I said. 'One that you can open.'

'You say a witch did this to me?' Bruno said. 'Which witch?'

'The one who gave you the chocolate bar in the hotel lobby yesterday,' I told him. 'Don't you remember?'

'The filthy old cow!' he shouted. 'I'll get her for this! Where is she? Who is she?'

'Forget it,' I said. 'You don't have a hope. Your biggest problem at the moment is your parents. How are they going to take this? Will they treat you with sympathy and kindness?'

Bruno considered this for a moment. 'I think,' he said, 'that my father is going to be a bit put out.'

'And your mother?'

'She's terrified of mice,' Bruno said.

'Then you've got a problem, haven't you?'

'Why only me?' he said. 'What about you?'

'My grandmother will understand perfectly,' I said. 'She knows all about witches.'

Bruno took another bite of his sandwich. 'What do you suggest?' he said.

'I suggest we both go first of all and consult my grandmother,' I said. 'She'll know exactly what to do.'

I moved towards the doors, which were standing open. Bruno, still grasping part of the sandwich in one paw, followed after me.

'When we get out into the corridor,' I said, 'we're going to run like mad. Stick close to the wall all the way and follow me. Do not talk and do not let anyone see you. Don't forget that just about anyone who catches sight of you will try to kill you.'

I snatched the sandwich out of his paw and threw it away. 'Here goes,' I said. 'Keep behind me.'

Chapter Fourteen

HELLO, GRANDMAMMA

As soon as I was out of the Ballroom, I took off like a flash. I streaked down the corridor, went through the Lounge and the Reading-Room and the Library and the Drawing-Room and came to the stairs. Up the stairs I went, jumping quite easily from one to the other, keeping well in against the wall all the time. 'Are you with me, Bruno?' I whispered.

'Right here,' he said.

My grandmother's room and my own were on the fifth floor. It was quite a climb, but we made it without meeting a single person on the way because everyone was using the lift. On the fifth floor, I raced along the corridor to the door of my grandmother's room. A pair of her shoes was standing outside the door to be cleaned. Bruno was alongside me. 'What do we do now?' he said.

Suddenly, I caught sight of a chambermaid coming along the corridor towards us. I saw at once that she was the one who had reported me to the Manager for keeping white mice. Not, therefore, the sort of person I wanted to meet in my present condition. 'Quick!' I said to Bruno. 'Hide in one of those shoes!' I hopped into one shoe and Bruno hopped into the other. I waited for the maid to walk past us. She didn't. When she came to the shoes, she bent down and picked them up. In doing this, she put her hand right inside the one I was hiding in. When one of her fingers touched me, I bit it. It was a silly thing to do, but I did it instinctively, without thinking. The maid let out a scream that must have been heard by ships far out in the English Channel, and she dropped the shoes and ran like the wind down the corridor.

My grandmother's door opened. 'What on earth is going on out here?' she said. I darted between her legs into her room and Bruno followed me.

'Close the door, Grandmamma!' I cried. 'Please hurry!'

She looked around and saw two small brown mice on the carpet. 'Please close it,' I said, and this time she actually saw me talking and recognized my voice. She froze and became absolutely motionless. Every part of her body, her fingers and hands and arms and head, became suddenly as stiff as a marble statue. Her face turned even paler than

marble and her eyes were stretched so wide I could see the whites all around them. Then she started to tremble. I thought she was going to faint and fall over.

103

'Please close the door quickly, Grandmamma,' I said. 'That awful maid might come in.'

She somehow managed to gather herself together enough to close the door. She leaned against it, staring down at me white-faced and shaking all over. I saw tears beginning to come out of her eyes and go dribbling down her cheeks.

'Don't cry, Grandmamma,' I said. 'Things could be a lot worse. I did get away from them. I'm still alive. So is Bruno.'

Very slowly, she bent down and picked me up with one hand. Then she picked Bruno up with the other hand and put us both on the table. There was a bowl of bananas in the centre of the table and Bruno jumped straight into it and began tearing away with his teeth at one of the banana skins to get at the fruit inside.

My grandmother grasped the arm of her chair to steady herself, but her eyes never left me.

'Sit down, dear Grandmamma,' I said.

She collapsed into her chair.

'Oh, my darling,' she murmured and now the tears were really streaming down her cheeks. 'Oh, my poor sweet darling. What *have* they done to you?'

'I know what they've done, Grandmamma, and I know what I am, but the funny thing is that I don't honestly feel especially bad about it. I don't even feel angry. In fact, I feel rather good. I know I'm not a boy any longer and I never will be again, but I'll be quite all right as long as there's always you to look after me.' I was not just trying to console her. I was being absolutely honest about the way I felt. You may think it odd that I wasn't weeping myself. It *was* odd. I simply can't explain it.

'Of course I'll look after you,' my grandmother murmured.

'Who is the other one?'

'That was a boy called Bruno Jenkins,' I told her. 'They got him first.'

My grandmother took a new long black cigar out of a case in her handbag and put it in her mouth. Then she got out a box of matches. She struck a match but her fingers were shaking so much that the flame kept missing the end of the cigar. When she got it lit at last, she took a long pull and sucked in the smoke. That seemed to calm her down a bit.

'Where did it happen?' she whispered. 'Where is the witch now? Is she in the hotel?'

'Grandmamma,' I said. 'It wasn't just one. It was *hundreds*! They're all over the place! They're right here in the hotel this very moment!'

She leaned forward and stared at me. 'You don't mean . . . you don't actually mean . . . you don't mean to tell me they're holding the Annual Meeting right here in the hotel?'

'They've held it, Grandmamma! It's finished! I heard it all! And all of them including The Grand High Witch herself are downstairs now! They're pretending they're the Royal Society for the Prevention of Cruelty to Children! They're all having tea with the Manager!'

'And they caught you?'

'They smelt me out,' I said.

'Dogs' droppings, was it?' she said, sighing.

'I'm afraid so. But it wasn't strong. They very nearly didn't smell me because I hadn't had a bath for ages.'

'Children should *never* have baths,' my grandmother said. 'It's a dangerous habit.'

'I agree, Grandmamma.'

She paused, sucking at her cigar.

'Do you *really* mean to tell me that they are now all downstairs having tea?' she said.

'I'm certain of it, Grandmamma.'

There was another pause. I could see the old glint of excitement slowly coming back into my grandmother's eyes, and all of a sudden she sat up very straight in her chair and said sharply, 'Tell me everything, right from the beginning. And please hurry.'

I took a deep breath and began to talk. I told about going to the Ballroom and hiding behind the screen to do my mouse-training.

106

I told about the notice saying Royal Society for the Prevention of Cruelty to Children. I told her all about the women coming in and sitting down and about the small woman who appeared on the stage and took off her mask. But when it came to describing what her face looked like underneath the mask, I simply couldn't find the right words. 'It was horrible, Grandmamma!' I said. 'Oh, it was so horrible! It was . . . it was like something that was going rotten!'

'Go on,' my grandmother said. 'Don't stop.'

Then I told her about all the others taking off their wigs and their gloves and their shoes, and how I saw before me a sea of bald pimply heads and how the women's fingers had little claws and how their feet had no toes.

My grandmother had come forward now in her armchair so that she was sitting right on the edge of it. Both her hands were cupped over the gold knob of the stick that she always used when walking, and she was staring at me with eyes as bright as two stars.

Then I told her how The Grand High Witch had shot out the fiery white-hot sparks and how they had turned one of the other witches into a puff of smoke.

'I've heard about that!' my grandmother cried out excitedly. 'But I never quite believed it! You are the first non-witch ever to see it happening! It is The Grand High Witch's most famous punishment! It is known as "getting fried", and all the other witches are petrified of having it done to them! I am told that The Grand High Witch makes it a rule to fry at least one witch at each Annual Meeting. She does it in order to keep the rest of them on their toes.'

'But they don't *have* any toes, Grandmamma.'

'I *know* they don't, my darling, but please go on.'

So then I told my grandmother about the Delayed Action Mouse-Maker, and when I came to the bit about turning all the children of England into mice, she actually leapt out of her chair shouting, 'I knew it! I knew they were brewing up something tremendous!'

'We've got to stop them,' I said.

She turned and stared at me. 'You can't stop witches,' she said. 'Just look at the power that terrible Grand High Witch has in her eyes alone! She could kill any of us at any time with those white-hot sparks of hers! You saw it yourself!'

'Even so, Grandmamma, we've still got to stop her from turning all the children of England into mice.'

'You haven't quite finished,' she said. 'Tell me about Bruno. How did they get *him*?'

So I described how Bruno Jenkins had come in and how I had actually seen him with my own eyes being shrunk into a mouse. My grandmother looked at Bruno, who was guzzling away in the bowl of bananas.

'Does he never stop eating?' she asked.

'Never,' I said. 'Can you explain something to me, Grandmamma?'

'I'll try,' she said. She reached out and lifted me off the table and put me on her lap. Very gently, she began stroking the soft fur along my back. It felt nice. 'What is it you want to ask me, my darling?' she said.

'The thing I don't understand,' I said, 'is how Bruno and I are still able to talk and think just as we did before.'

'It's quite simple,' my grandmother said. 'All they've done is to shrink you and give you four legs and a furry coat, but they haven't been able to change you into a one hundred per cent mouse. You are still yourself in everything except your appearance. You've still got your own mind and your own brain and your own voice, and thank goodness for that.'

'So I'm not really an *ordinary* mouse at all,' I said. 'I'm a sort of mouse-person.'

'Quite right,' she said. 'You are a human in mouse's clothing. You are very special.'

We sat there in silence for a few moments while my grandmother went on stroking me very gently with one finger and puffing her cigar with the other hand. The only sound in the room was made by Bruno as he attacked the bananas in the bowl. But I wasn't doing nothing as I lay there on her lap. I was thinking like mad. My brain was whizzing as it had never whizzed before.

'Grandmamma,' I said. 'I may have a bit of an idea.'

'Yes, my darling. What is it?'

'The Grand High Witch told them her room was number 454. Right?'

'Right,' she said.

'Well, *my* room is number 554. Mine, 554, is on the fifth floor, so hers, 454, will be on the fourth floor.'

'That is correct,' my grandmother said.

'Then don't you think it's possible that room 454 is directly underneath room 554?'

'That's more than likely,' she said. 'These modern hotels are all built like boxes of bricks. But what if it is?'

'Would you please take me out on to my balcony so I can look down,' I said.

All the rooms in the Hotel Magnificent had small private balconies. My grandmother carried me through into my own bedroom and out on to my balcony. We both peered down to the balcony immediately below.

'Now if that *is* her room,' I said, 'then I'll bet I could climb down there somehow and get in.'

'And get caught all over again,' my grandmother said. 'I won't allow it.'

'At this moment,' I said, 'all the witches are down on the Sunshine Terrace having tea with the Manager. The Grand High Witch probably won't be back until six o'clock or just before. That's when she's going to dish out supplies of that foul formula to the ancient ones who are too old to climb trees after gruntles' eggs.'

'And what if you did manage to get into her room?' my grandmother said. 'What then?'

'Then I should try to find the place where she keeps her supply of Delayed Action Mouse-Maker, and if I succeeded then I would steal one bottle of it and bring it back here.'

'Could you carry it?'

'I think so,' I said. 'It's a very small bottle.'

'I'm frightened of that stuff,' my grandmother said. 'What would you do with it if you did manage to get it?'

'One bottle is enough for five hundred people,' I said. 'That would give each and every witch down there a double dose at least. We could turn them all into mice.'

My grandmother jumped about an inch in the air. We were out on my balcony and there was a drop of about a million feet below us and I very nearly bounced out of her hand over the railings when she jumped.

'Be careful with me, Grandmamma,' I said.

'What an idea!' she cried. 'It's fantastic! It's tremendous! You're a genius, my darling!'

'Wouldn't it be something?' I said. 'Wouldn't that really be something?'

'We'd get rid of every witch in England in one swoop!' she cried. '*And* The Grand High Witch into the bargain!'

'We've got to try it,' I said.

'Listen,' she said, nearly dropping me over the balcony once again in her excitement. 'If we brought this off, it would be the greatest triumph in the whole history of witchery!'

'There's a lot of work to do,' I said.

'Of course there's a lot of work to do,' she said. 'Just for a start, supposing you did manage to get hold of one of those bottles, how would you get it into their food?'

'We'll work that out later,' I said. 'Let's try to get the stuff first.

How can we find out for sure if that's her room just below us?'

'We shall check it out immediately!' my grandmother cried. 'Come along! There's not a second to waste!' Carrying me in one hand, she went bustling out of the bedroom and along the corridor, banging her stick on the carpet with each step she took. We went down the stairs one flight to the fourth floor. The bedrooms on either side of the corridor had their numbers painted on the doors in gold.

'Here it is!' my grandmother cried. 'Number 454.' She tried the door. It was locked of course. She looked up and down the long empty hotel corridor. 'I do believe you're right,' she said. 'This room is almost certainly directly below yours.' She marched back

along the corridor, counting the number of doors from The Grand High Witch's room to the staircase. There were six.

She climbed back up to the fifth floor and repeated the exercise.

'She *is* directly below you!' my grandmother cried out. 'Her room is right below yours!'

She carried me back into my own bedroom and went out once again on to the balcony. 'That's her balcony down there,' she said. 'And what's more, the door from her balcony into her bedroom is wide open! How are you going to climb down?'

'I don't know,' I said. Our rooms were in the front of the hotel and they looked down on to the beach and the sea. Immediately below my balcony, thousands of feet below, I could see a fence of spiked railings. If I fell, I'd be a gonner.

'I've got it!' my grandmother cried. With me in her hand, she rushed back into her own room and began rummaging in the chest-of-drawers. She came out with a ball of blue knitting-wool. One end of it was attached to some needles and a half-finished sock she had been knitting for me. 'This is perfect,' she said. 'I shall put you in the sock and lower you down on to The Grand High Witch's balcony. But we *must* hurry! Any moment now that monster will be returning to her room!'

Chapter Fifteen

THE MOUSE-BURGLAR

My grandmother hustled me back into my own bedroom and out on to the balcony. 'Are you ready?' she asked. 'I'm going to put you in the sock now.'

'I hope I can manage this,' I said. 'I'm only a little mouse.'

'You'll manage,' she said. 'Good luck, my darling.' She popped me into the sock and started lowering me over the balcony. I crouched inside the sock and held my breath. Through the stitches I could see out quite clearly. Miles below me, the children playing on the beach were the size of beetles. The sock started swinging in the breeze. I looked up and saw my grandmother's head sticking out over the railings of the balcony above. 'You're nearly there!' she called out. 'Here we go! Gently does it. You're down!'

I felt a slight bump. 'In you go!' my grandmother was shouting. 'Hurry, hurry, hurry! Search the room!'

I jumped out of the sock and ran into The Grand High Witch's bedroom. There was the same musty smell about the place that I had noticed in the Ballroom. It was the stench of witches. It reminded me of the smell inside the men's public lavatory at our local railway-station.

As far as I could see, the room was tidy enough. There was no sign anywhere that it was inhabited by anyone but an ordinary person. But then there wouldn't be, would there? No witch would be stupid enough to leave anything suspicious lying around for the hotel maid to see.

Suddenly I saw a frog jumping across the carpet and disappearing under the bed. I jumped myself.

'*Hurry up!*' came my grandmother's voice from somewhere high up outside. 'Grab the stuff and *get out*!'

I started skittering round and trying to search the room. This wasn't so easy. I couldn't, for example, open any of the drawers. I couldn't open the doors of the big wardrobe either. I stopped skittering about. I sat in the middle of the floor and had a think. If The Grand High Witch wanted to hide something top secret, where would she put it? Certainly not in any ordinary drawer. Not in the wardrobe either. It was too obvious. I jumped up on to the bed to get a better view of the room. *Hey*, I thought, *what about under the mattress?* Very carefully, I lowered myself over the edge of the bed and wormed my way underneath the mattress. I had to push forward hard to make any headway, but I kept at it. I couldn't see a thing. I was scrabbling about under the mattress when my head suddenly bumped against something hard *inside* the mattress above me. I reached up and felt it with my paw. Could it be a little bottle?

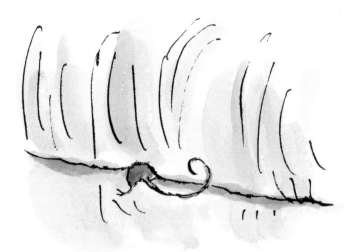

It *was* a little bottle! I could trace the shape of it through the cloth of the mattress. And right alongside it, I felt another hard lump, and another and another. The Grand High Witch must have slit open the mattress and put all the bottles inside and then sewn it all up again. I began tearing away frantically at the mattress cloth above my head with my teeth. My front teeth were extremely sharp and it didn't take me long to make a small hole. I climbed into the hole and grabbed a bottle by the neck. I pushed it down through the hole in the mattress and climbed out after it.

Walking backwards and dragging the bottle behind me, I managed to reach the edge of the mattress. I rolled the bottle off the bed on to the carpet. It bounced but it didn't break. I jumped down off the bed. I examined the little bottle. It was identical to the one The Grand High Witch had had in the Ballroom. There was a label on this one. FORMULA 86, it said. DELAYED ACTION MOUSE-MAKER. Then it said, *This bottle contains five hundred doses*. Eureka! I felt tremendously pleased with myself.

Three frogs came hopping out from under the bed. They crouched on the carpet, staring at me with large black eyes. I stared

back at them. Those huge eyes were the saddest things I had ever seen. It suddenly occurred to me that almost certainly once upon a time they had been children, those frogs, before The Grand High

Witch had got hold of them. I stood there clutching the bottle and staring at the frogs. 'Who are you?' I asked them.

At that exact moment, I heard a key turning in the lock of the door and the door burst open and The Grand High Witch swept into the room. The frogs jumped underneath the bed again in one quick hop. I darted after them, still clutching the bottle, and I ran back against the wall and squeezed in behind one of the bedposts. I heard feet walking on the carpet. I peeped round the bedpost. The three frogs were clustered together under the middle of the bed. Frogs cannot hide like mice. They cannot run like mice, either. All they can do, poor things, is to hop about rather clumsily.

Suddenly The Grand High Witch's face came into view, peering under the bed. I popped my head back behind the bedpost.

'So there you are, my little frrroggies,' I heard her saying. 'You can stay vhere you are until I go to bed tonight, then I shall thrrrow you out of the vindow and the seagulls can have you for supper.'

Suddenly very loud and clear there came the sound of my grandmother's voice through the open balcony door. 'Hurry up, my darling!' it shouted. 'Do hurry up! You'd better come out quickly!'

'Who is calling?' snapped The Grand High Witch. I peeped round the bedpost again and saw her walking across the carpet to the balcony door. 'Who is this on my balcony?' she muttered. 'Who is it? Who dares to trrrespass on my balcony?' She went through the door on to the balcony itself.

'Vot is this knitting-vool hanging down here?' I heard her saying.

'Oh, hello,' came my grandmother's voice. 'I just dropped my knitting over the balcony by mistake. But it's all right. I've got hold of one end of it. I can pull it up by myself, thank you all the same.' I marvelled at the coolness of her voice.

'Who vur you talking to just now?' snapped The Grand High Witch. 'Who vur you telling to hurry up and come out qvickly?'

'I was talking to my little grandson,' I heard my grandmother saying. 'He's been in the bathroom for hours and it's time he came out. He sits in there reading books and he forgets completely where he is! Do *you* have any children, my dear?'

'I do not!' shouted The Grand High Witch, and she came quickly back into the bedroom, *slamming the balcony door behind her.*

I was cooked. My escape route was closed. I was shut up in the room with The Grand High Witch and three terrified frogs. I was just as terrified as the frogs. I was quite sure that if I was spotted, I would be caught and thrown out over the balcony for the seagulls.

There came a knock on the bedroom door. 'Vot is it this time?' shouted The Grand High Witch.

'It is we ancient ones,' said a meek voice from behind the door. 'It is six o'clock and we have come to collect the bottles that you promised us, O Your Grandness.'

I saw her crossing the carpet towards the door. The door was opened and then I saw a whole lot of feet and shoes beginning to enter the room. They were coming in slowly and hesitantly, as though the owners of those shoes were frightened of entering. 'Come in! Come in!' snapped The Grand High Witch. 'Do not stand out there dithering in the corrri-dor! I don't have all night!'

I saw my chance. I jumped out from behind the bedpost and ran like lightning towards the open door. I jumped over several pairs of shoes on the way and in three seconds I was out in the

corridor, still clutching the precious bottle to my chest. No one had seen me. There were no shouts of *Mouse! Mouse!* All I could hear were the voices of the ancient witches burbling their silly sentences about 'How kind Your Grandness is' and all the rest of it. I went scampering down the corridor to the stairs and up one flight. I went to the fifth floor and then along the corridor again until I came to the door of my own bedroom. Thank goodness there was no one in sight. Using the bottom of the little bottle, I began tap-tap-tapping on the door. *Tap tap tap tap*, I went. *Tap tap tap . . . tap tap tap . . .* Would my grandmother hear me? I thought that she must. The bottle made quite a loud tap each time it struck. *Tap tap tap . . . tap tap tap . . .* Just so long as nobody came along the corridor.

But the door didn't open. I decided to take a risk. 'Grandmamma!' I shouted as loudly as I possibly could. 'Grandmamma! It's me! Let me in!'

I heard her feet coming across the carpet and the door opened. I went in like an arrow. 'I've done it!' I cried, jumping up and down. 'I've got it, Grandmamma! Look, here it is! I've got a whole bottle of it!'

She closed the door. She bent down and picked me up and hugged me. 'Oh, my darling!' she cried. 'Thank heavens you're safe!' She took the little bottle from me and read the label aloud. '"Formula 86 Delayed Action Mouse-Maker!"' she read. '"This bottle contains five hundred doses!" You brilliant darling boy! You're a wonder! You're a marvel! How on earth did you get out of her room?'

'I nipped out when the ancient witches were coming in,' I told her. 'It was all a bit hairy, Grandmamma. I wouldn't want to do it again.'

'I saw her too!' my grandmother said.

'I know you did, Grandmamma. I heard you talking to each other. Didn't you think she was absolutely foul?'

'She's a murderer,' my grandmother said. 'She's the most evil woman in the entire world!'

'Did you see her mask?' I asked.

'It's amazing,' my grandmother said. 'It looks just like a real face. Even though I knew it was a mask, I still couldn't tell. Oh, my darling!' she cried, giving me a hug. 'I thought I'd never see you again! I'm so happy you got away!'

Chapter Sixteen

MR AND MRS JENKINS
MEET BRUNO

*M*y grandmother carried me back into her own bedroom and put me on the table. She set the precious bottle down beside me. 'What time are those witches having supper in the Dining-Room?' she asked.

'Eight o'clock,' I said.

She looked at her watch. 'It is now ten-past six,' she said. 'We've got until eight o'clock to work out our next move.' Suddenly, her eye fell upon Bruno. He was still in the banana bowl on the table. He had eaten three bananas and was now attacking a fourth. He had become immensely fat.

'That's quite enough,' my grandmother said, lifting him out of the bowl and putting him on the table-top. 'I think it's time we returned this little fellow to the bosom of his family. Don't you agree, Bruno?'

Bruno scowled at her. I had never seen a mouse scowl before, but he managed it. 'My parents let me eat as much as I want,' he said. 'I'd rather be with them than with you.'

'Of course you would,' my grandmother said. 'Do you know where your parents might be at this moment?'

'They were in the Lounge not long ago,' I said. 'I saw them sitting there as we dashed through on our way up here.'

'Right,' my grandmother said. 'Let's go and see if they are still there. Do you want to come along?' she added, looking at me.

'Yes, please,' I said.

'I shall put you both in my handbag,' she said. 'Keep quiet and stay out of sight. If you must peep out now and again, don't show more than your nose.'

Her handbag was a large bulgy black-leather affair with a tortoise-shell clasp. She picked up Bruno and me and popped us into it. 'I shall leave the clasp undone,' she said. 'But be sure to keep out of sight.'

I had no intention of keeping out of sight. I wanted to see everything. I seated myself in a little side-pocket inside the bag, near the clasp, and from there I was able to poke my head out whenever I wanted to.

'Hey!' Bruno called out. 'Give me the rest of that banana I was eating.'

'Oh all right,' my grandmother said. 'Anything to keep you quiet.' She dropped the half-eaten banana into the bag, then slung the bag over her arm and marched out of the room and went thumping along the corridor with her walking-stick.

We went down in the lift to the ground floor and made our way through the Reading-Room to the Lounge. And there, sure enough, sat Mr and Mrs Jenkins in a couple of armchairs with a low round glass-covered table between them. There were several other groups in there as well, but the Jenkinses were the only couple sitting alone.

Mr Jenkins was reading a newspaper. Mrs Jenkins was knitting something large and mustard-coloured. Only my nose and eyes were above the clasp of my grandmother's handbag, but I had a super view. I could see everything.

My grandmother, dressed in black lace, went thumping across the floor of the Lounge and halted in front of the Jenkinses' table. 'Are you Mr and Mrs Jenkins?' she asked.

Mr Jenkins looked at her over the top of his newspaper and frowned. 'Yes,' he said. 'I am Mr Jenkins. What can I do for you, madam?'

'I'm afraid I have some rather alarming news for you,' she said. 'It's about your son, Bruno.'

'What about Bruno?' Mr Jenkins said.

Mrs Jenkins looked up but went on knitting. 'What's the little blighter been up to now?' Mr Jenkins asked. 'Raiding the kitchen, I suppose.'

'It's a bit worse than that,' my grandmother said. 'Do you think we might go somewhere more private while I tell you about it?'

'Private?' Mr Jenkins said. 'Why do we have to be private?'

'This is not an easy thing for me to explain,' my grandmother said. 'I'd much rather we all went up to your room and sat down before I tell you any more.'

Mr Jenkins lowered his paper. Mrs Jenkins stopped knitting. 'I don't *want* to go up to my room, madam,' Mr Jenkins said. 'I'm quite comfortable here, thank you very much.' He was a large coarse man and he wasn't used to being pushed around by anybody. 'Kindly state your business and then leave us alone,' he added. He spoke as though he was addressing someone who was trying to sell him a vacuum-cleaner at the back door.

My poor grandmother, who had been doing her best to be as kind to them as possible, now began to bristle a bit herself. 'We really can't talk in here,' she said. 'There are too many people. This is a rather delicate and personal matter.'

'I'll talk where I dashed well want to, madam,' Mr Jenkins said. 'Come on now, out with it! If Bruno has broken a window or smashed your spectacles, then I'll pay for the damage, but I'm not budging out of this seat!'

One or two other groups in the room were beginning to stare at us now.

'Where *is* Bruno anyway?' Mr Jenkins said. 'Tell him to come here and see me.'

'He's here already,' my grandmother said. 'He's in my handbag.'

She patted the big floppy leather bag with her walking-stick.

'What the heck d'you mean he's in your handbag?' Mr Jenkins shouted.

'Are you trying to be funny?' Mrs Jenkins said, very prim.

'There's nothing funny about this,' my grandmother said. 'Your son has suffered a rather unfortunate mishap.'

'He's always suffering mishaps,' Mr Jenkins said. 'He suffers from overeating and then he suffers from wind. You should hear him after supper. He sounds like a brass band! But a good dose of castor-oil soon puts him right again. Where is the little beggar?'

'I've already told you,' my grandmother said. 'He's in my handbag. But I do think it might be better if we went somewhere private before you meet him in his present state.'

'This woman's mad,' Mrs Jenkins said. 'Tell her to go away.'

'The plain fact is,' my grandmother said, 'that your son Bruno has been rather drastically altered.'

'*Altered!*' shouted Mr Jenkins. 'What the devil d'you mean *altered*?'

'Go away!' Mrs Jenkins said. 'You're a silly old woman!'

'I am trying to tell you as gently as I possibly can that Bruno really is in my handbag,' my grandmother said. 'My own grandson actually saw them doing it to him.'

'Saw *who* doing *what* to him, for heaven's sake?' shouted Mr Jenkins. He had a black moustache which jumped up and down when he shouted.

'Saw the witches turning him into a mouse,' my grandmother said.

'Call the Manager, dear,' Mrs Jenkins said to her husband. 'Have this mad woman thrown out of the hotel.'

At this point, my grandmother's patience came to an end. She fished around in her handbag and found Bruno. She lifted him out and dumped him on the glass-topped table. Mrs Jenkins took one look at the fat little brown mouse who was still chewing a bit of banana and she let out a shriek that rattled the crystals on the chandelier. She sprang out of her chair yelling, 'It's a mouse! Take it away! I can't stand the things!'

'It's Bruno,' my grandmother said.

'You nasty cheeky old woman!' shouted Mr Jenkins. He started flapping his newspaper at Bruno, trying to sweep him off the table. My grandmother rushed forward and managed to grab hold of him before he was swept away. Mrs Jenkins was still screaming her head off and Mr Jenkins was towering over us and shouting, 'Get out of here! How dare you frighten my wife like that! Take your filthy mouse away this instant!'

'Help!' screamed Mrs Jenkins. Her face had gone the colour of the underside of a fish.

'Well, I did my best,' my grandmother said, and with that she turned and sailed out of the room, carrying Bruno with her.

Chapter Seventeen

The Plan

When we got back to the bedroom, my grandmother took both me and Bruno out of her handbag and put us on the table. 'Why on earth didn't you speak up and tell your father who you were?' she said to Bruno.

'Because I had my mouth full,' Bruno said. He jumped straight back into the bowl of bananas and went on with his eating.

'What a very disagreeable little boy you are,' my grandmother said to him.

'Not boy,' I said. 'Mouse.'

'Quite right, my darling. But we don't have time to worry about him at this moment. We have plans to make. In about an hour and a half's time, all the witches will be going down to supper in the Dining-Room. Right?'

'Right,' I said.

'And every one of them has got to be given a dose of Mouse-Maker,' she said. 'How on earth are we going to do that?'

'Grandmamma,' I said. 'I think you are forgetting that a mouse can go places where human beings can't.'

'That's quite right,' she said. 'But even a mouse can't go creeping around on the table-top carrying a bottle and sprinkling Mouse-Maker all over the witches' roast beef without being spotted.'

'I wasn't thinking of doing it in the Dining-Room,' I said.

'Then where?' she asked.

'In the kitchen,' I said, 'while their food is being got ready.'

My grandmother stared at me. 'My darling child,' she said slowly, 'I do believe that turning you into a mouse has doubled your brain-power!'

'A little mouse,' I said, 'can go scuttling round the kitchen among the pots and pans, and if he's very careful no one will ever see him.'

'Brilliant!' my grandmother cried out. 'By golly, I think you've got it!'

'The only thing is,' I said, 'how will I know which food is theirs? I don't want to put it in the wrong saucepan. It would be disastrous if I turned all the other guests into mice by mistake, and especially you, Grandmamma.'

'Then you'll just have to creep into the kitchen and find a good hiding-place and wait . . . and listen. Just lie there in some dark cranny listening and listening to what the cooks are saying . . . and then, with a bit of luck, somebody's going to give you a clue. Whenever they have a very big party to cook for, the food is always prepared separately.'

'Right,' I said. 'That's what I'll have to do. I shall wait there and I shall listen and I shall hope for a bit of luck.'

'It's going to be very dangerous,' my grandmother said. 'Nobody welcomes a mouse in the kitchen. If they see you, they'll squash you to death.'

'I won't let them see me,' I said.

'Don't forget you'll be carrying the bottle,' she said, 'so you won't be nearly so quick and nippy.'

'I can run quite fast standing up with the bottle in my arms,' I said. 'I did it just now, don't you remember? I came all the way up from The Grand High Witch's room carrying it.'

'What about unscrewing the top?' she said. 'That might be difficult for you.'

'Let me try,' I said. I took hold of the little bottle and using both
my front paws, I found I was able to unscrew the cap quite easily.

'That's great,' my grandmother said. 'You really are a very
clever mouse.' She glanced at her watch. 'At half-past seven,' she
said, 'I shall go down to the Dining-Room for supper with you in
my handbag. I shall then release you under the table together with
the precious bottle and from then on you'll be on your own. You
will have to work your way unseen across the Dining-Room to the
door that leads into the kitchen. There will be waiters going in and
out of that door all the time. You will have to choose the right
moment and nip in behind one of them, but for heaven's sake be
sure that you don't get trodden on or squeezed in the door.'

'I'll try not to,' I said.

'And whatever happens, you mustn't let them catch you.'

'Don't go on about it, Grandmamma. You're making
me nervous.'

'You're a brave little fellow,' she said. 'I do love you.'

'What shall we do with Bruno?' I asked her.

Bruno looked up. 'I'm coming with you,' he said, speaking with his mouth full of banana. 'I'm not going to miss my supper!'

My grandmother considered this for a moment. 'I'll take you along,' she said, 'if you promise to stay in my bag and keep absolutely silent.'

'Will you pass food down to me from the table?' Bruno asked.

'Yes,' she said, 'if you promise to behave yourself. Would *you* like something to eat, my darling?' she said to me.

'No, thank you,' I said. 'I'm too excited to eat. And I've got to keep fit and frisky for the big job ahead.'

'It's a big job all right,' my grandmother said. 'You'll never do a bigger one.'

Chapter Eighteen

IN THE KITCHEN

'The time has come!' my grandmother said. 'The great moment has arrived! Are you ready, my darling?'

It was exactly half-past seven. Bruno was in the bowl finishing that fourth banana. 'Hang on,' he said. 'Just a few more bites.'

'No!' my grandmother said. 'We've got to go!' She picked him up and held him tight in her hand. She was very tense and nervous. I had never seen her like that before. 'I'm going to put you both in my handbag now,' she said, 'but I shall leave the clasp undone.' She popped Bruno into it first. I waited, clutching the little bottle to my chest. 'Now you,' she said. She picked me up and gave me a kiss on the nose. 'Good luck, my darling. Oh, by the way, you do realize you've got a tail, don't you?'

'A what?' I said.

'A tail. A long curly tail.'

'I must say that never occurred to me,' I said. 'Good gracious me, so I have! I can see it now! I can actually move it! It is rather grand, isn't it?'

'I mention it only because it might come in useful when you're climbing about in the kitchen,' my grandmother said. 'You can curl it around and you can hook it on to things and you can swing from it and lower yourself to the ground from high places.'

'I wish I'd known this before,' I said. 'I could have practised using it.'

'Too late now,' my grandmother said. 'We've got to go.' She popped me into her handbag with Bruno, and at once I took up my usual perch in the small side-pocket so that I could poke my head out and see what was going on.

My grandmother picked up her walking-stick and out she went into the corridor to the lift. She pressed the button and the lift came up and she got in. There was no one in there with us.

'Listen,' she said. 'I won't be able to talk to you much once we're in the Dining-Room. If I do, people will think I'm dotty and talking to myself.'

The lift reached the ground floor and stopped with a jerk. My grandmother walked out of it and crossed the lobby of the hotel and entered the Dining-Room. It was a huge room with gold decorations on the ceiling and big mirrors around the walls. The regular guests always had their tables reserved for them and most of them were already in their places and starting to eat their suppers. Waiters were buzzing about all over the place, carrying plates and dishes. Our table was a small one beside the right-hand wall about halfway down the room. My grandmother made her way to it and sat down.

Peeping out of the handbag, I could see in the very centre of the room two long tables that were not yet occupied. Each of them carried a notice fixed on to a sort of silver stick and the notices said, RESERVED FOR MEMBERS OF THE RSPCC.

My grandmother looked towards the long tables but said nothing. She unfolded her napkin and spread it over the handbag on her lap. Her hand slid under the napkin and took hold of me gently. With the napkin covering me, she lifted me up close to her face and whispered, 'I am about to put you on the floor under the table. The table-cloth reaches almost to the ground so no one will see you. Have you got hold of the bottle?'

'Yes,' I whispered back. 'I'm ready, Grandmamma.'

Just then, a waiter in a black suit came and stood by our table.

I could see his legs from under the napkin and as soon as I heard his voice, I knew who he was. His name was William. 'Good evening, madam,' he said to my grandmother. 'Where is the little gentleman tonight?'

'He's not feeling very well,' my grandmother said. 'He's staying in his room.'

'I'm sorry to hear that,' William said. 'Today there is green-pea soup to start with, and for the main course you have a choice of either grilled fillet of sole or roast lamb.'

'Pea soup and lamb for me, please,' my grandmother said. 'But don't hurry it, William. I'm in no rush tonight. In fact, you can bring me a glass of dry sherry first.'

'Of course, madam,' William said, and he went away.

My grandmother pretended she had dropped something, and as she bent down, she slid me out from under the napkin on to the floor under the table. 'Go, darling, go!' she whispered, then she straightened up again.

I was on my own now. I stood clasping the little bottle. I knew exactly where the door into the kitchen was. I had to go about halfway round the enormous Dining-Room to reach it. Here goes, I thought, and like a flash I skittled out from under the table and made for the wall. I had no intention of going across the Dining-Room floor. It was far too risky. My plan was to cling close to the skirting of the wall all the way round until I reached the kitchen door.

I ran. Oh, how I ran. I don't think anyone saw me. They were all too busy eating. But to reach the door leading to the kitchen I had to cross the main entrance to the Dining-Room. I was just about to do this when in poured a great flood of females. I pressed myself against the wall clutching the bottle. At first I saw only the

shoes and ankles of these women who were surging in through the door, but when I glanced up a bit higher I knew at once who they were. They were the witches coming in to dinner!

I waited until they had all passed me by, then I dashed on towards the kitchen door. A waiter opened it to go in. I nipped in after him and hid behind a big garbage-bin on the floor. I stayed there for several minutes, just listening to all the talk and the racket. By golly, what a place that kitchen was! The noise! And the steam! And the clatter of pots and pans! And the cooks all shouting! And the waiters all rushing in and out from the Dining-Room yelling the food orders to the cooks! 'Four soups and two lambs and two fish

for table twenty-eight! Three apple-pies and two strawberry ice-creams for number seventeen!' Stuff like that going on all the time.

Not far above my head there was a handle sticking out from the side of the garbage-bin. Still clutching the bottle, I gave a leap, turned a somersault in the air, and caught hold of the handle with the end of my tail. Suddenly there I was swinging to and fro upside down. It was terrific. I loved it. *This*, I told myself, *is how a trapeze artist in a circus must feel as he goes swishing through the air high up in the circus tent.* The only difference was that his trapeze could only swing backwards and forwards. My trapeze (my tail) could swing me in any direction I wanted. Perhaps I would become a circus mouse after all.

Just then, a waiter came in with a plate in his hand and I heard him saying, 'The old hag on table fourteen says this meat is too tough! She wants another portion!' One of the cooks said, 'Gimme her plate!' I dropped to the floor and peeped round the garbage-bin. I saw the cook scrape the meat off the plate and slap another bit on. Then he said, 'Come on, boys, give her some gravy!' He carried the plate round to everyone in the kitchen and do you know what they did? Every one of those cooks and kitchen-boys spat on to the old lady's plate! 'See how she likes it now!' said the cook, handing the plate back to the waiter.

Quite soon another waiter came in and he shouted, 'Everyone in the big RSPCC party wants the soup!' That's when I started sitting up and taking notice. I was all ears now. I edged a bit further round the garbage-bin so that I could see everything that was going on in the kitchen. A man with a tall white hat who must have been the head chef shouted, 'Put the soup for the big party in the larger silver soup-tureen!'

I saw the head chef place a huge silver basin on to the wooden side-bench that ran along the whole length of the kitchen against the opposite wall. *Into that silver basin is where the soup is going*, I told myself. *So that's where the stuff in my little bottle must go as well.*

I noticed that high up near the ceiling, above the side-bench, there was a long shelf crammed with saucepans and frying-pans. *If I can somehow clamber up on to that shelf*, I thought, *then I've got it made. I shall be directly above the silver basin.*

But first I must somehow get across to the other side of the kitchen and then up on to the middle shelf. A great idea came to me! Once again, I jumped up and hooked my tail around the handle of the garbage-bin. Then, hanging upside down, I began to swing. Higher and higher I swung. I was remembering the trapeze artist in the circus I had seen last Easter and the way he had got the trapeze swinging higher and higher and higher and had then let go and gone flying through the air. So just at the right moment, at the top of my swing, I let go with my tail and went soaring clear across the kitchen and made a perfect landing on the middle shelf!

By golly, I thought, *what marvellous things a mouse can do! And I'm only a beginner!*

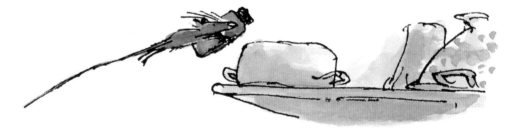

No one had seen me. They were all far too busy with their pots and pans. From the middle shelf I somehow managed to shinny up a little water-pipe in the corner, and in no time at all I was up on the very top shelf just under the ceiling, among all the saucepans and the frying-pans. I knew that no one could possibly see me up there. It was a super position, and I began working my way along the shelf until I was directly above the big empty silver basin they were going to pour the soup into. I put down my bottle. I unscrewed the top and crept to the edge of the shelf and quickly poured what was in it straight into the silver basin below. The next moment, one

of the cooks came along with a gigantic saucepan of steaming green soup and poured the whole lot into the silver basin. He put the lid on the basin and shouted, 'Soup for the big party all ready to go out!' Then a waiter arrived and carried the silver basin away.

I had done it! Even if I never got back alive to my grandmother, the witches were still going to get the Mouse-Maker! I left the empty bottle behind a large saucepan and began working my way back along the top shelf. It was much easier to move about without the bottle. I began using my tail more and more. I swung from the handle of one saucepan to the handle of another all the way along that top shelf, while far below me cooks and waiters were all bustling about and kettles were steaming and pans were spluttering and pots were boiling and I thought to myself, *Oh boy, this is the life! What fun it is to be a mouse doing an exciting job like this!* I kept right on swinging. I swung most marvellously from handle to handle, and I was enjoying myself so much that I completely forgot I was in full view of anyone in the kitchen who might happen to glance upwards. What came next happened so quickly I had no time to save myself. I heard a man's voice yelling, 'A mouse! Look at that dirty little mouse!' And I caught a glimpse below me of a white-coated figure in a tall white hat and then there was a flash of steel

as the carving-knife whizzed through the air and there was a shoot of pain in the end of my tail and suddenly I was falling and falling head-first towards the floor.

Even as I fell, I knew just what had happened. I knew that the tip of my tail had been cut off and that I was about to crash on to the floor and everyone in the kitchen would be after me. 'A mouse!' they were shouting. 'A mouse! A mouse! Catch it quick!' I hit the floor and jumped up and ran for my life. All around me there were big black boots going *stamp stamp stamp* and I dodged around them and ran and ran and ran, twisting and turning, and dodging and swerving across the kitchen floor. 'Get it!' they were shouting. 'Kill it! Stamp on it!' The whole floor seemed to be full of black boots stamping away at me and I dodged and swerved and twisted and turned and then in sheer desperation, hardly knowing what I was doing, wanting only a place to hide, I ran up the trouser-leg of one of the cooks and clung to his sock!

'Hey!' the cook shouted. 'Jeepers creepers! He's gone up my trouser! Hold on, boys! I'll get him this time!'

The man's hands began slap-slapping at the trouser-leg and now I really *was* going to get smashed if I didn't move quickly. There was only one way to go and that was up. I dug my little claws into the hairy skin of the man's leg and scuttled upwards, higher and higher, past the calf and past the knee and on to the thigh.

'Holy smoke!' the man was yelling. 'It's going all the way up! It's going right up my leg!' I heard shrieks of laughter coming from the other cooks but I can promise you I wasn't laughing myself. I was running for my life. The man's hands were slap-slap-slapping all around me and he was jumping up and down as though he was standing on hot bricks, and I kept climbing and I kept dodging and very soon I reached the very top of the trouser-leg and there was nowhere else to go.

'Help! Help! Help!' the man was screaming. 'It's in my knickers! It's running round in my flaming knickers! Get it out! Someone help me to get it out!'

'Take off your trousers, you silly slob!' someone else shouted. 'Pull down your pants and we'll soon catch him!'

I was in the middle of the man's trousers now, in the place where the two trouser-legs meet and the zip begins. It was dark and awfully hot in there. I knew I had to keep going. I dashed onward and found the top of the other trouser-leg. I went down it like greased lightning and came out at the bottom of it and once again I was on the floor. I heard the stupid cook still shouting, 'It's in my trousers! Get it out! Will somebody *please* help me to get it out before it bites me!' I caught a flashing glimpse of the entire kitchen staff crowding round him and laughing their heads off and nobody saw the little brown mouse as it flew across the floor and dived into a sack of potatoes.

I burrowed down in among the dirty potatoes and held my breath.

The cook must have started taking his trousers right off because now they were shouting, 'It's not in there! There's no mice in there, you silly twerp!'

'There was! I swear there was!' the man was shouting back. 'You've never *had* a mouse in your trousers! You don't know what it feels like!'

The fact that a tiny little creature like me had caused such a commotion among a bunch of grown-up men gave me a happy feeling. I couldn't help smiling in spite of the pain in my tail.

I stayed where I was until I was sure they had forgotten about me. Then I crept out of the potatoes and cautiously poked my tiny head over the edge of the sack. Once again the kitchen was all of a bustle with cooks and waiters rushing about everywhere. I saw the waiter who had come in earlier with the complaint about tough meat coming in again. 'Hey, boys!' he shouted. 'I asked the old hag if the new bit of meat was any better and she said it was perfectly delicious! She said it was really tasty!'

I had to get out of that kitchen and back to my grandmother. There was only one way to do this. I must make a dash clear across the floor and out through the door behind one of the waiters. I stayed quite still, watching for my chance. My tail was hurting terribly. I curled it round so as to have a look at it. About two inches of it were missing and it was bleeding quite a lot.

There was a waiter loading up with a batch of plates full of pink ice-cream. He had a plate in each hand and two more balanced on each arm. He went towards the door. He pushed it open with his shoulder. I leapt out of the sack of potatoes and went across that kitchen floor and into the Dining-Room like a streak of light, and I didn't stop running until I was underneath my grandmother's table.

It was lovely to see my grandmother's feet again in those old-fashioned black shoes with their straps and buttons. I shinnied up one of her legs and landed on her lap. 'Hello, Grandmamma!' I whispered. 'I'm back! I did it! I poured it all into their soup!'

Her hand came down and caressed me. 'Well *done*, my darling!' she whispered back. 'Well done you! They are at this very moment eating that soup!' Suddenly, she withdrew her hand. 'You're bleeding!' she whispered. 'My darling, what's happened to you?'

'One of the cooks cut off my tail with a carving-knife,' I whispered back. 'It hurts like billy-o.'

'Let me look at it,' she said. She bent her head and examined my tail. 'You poor little thing,' she whispered. 'I'm going to bandage it up with my handkerchief. That will stop the bleeding.'

She fished a small lace-edged handkerchief out of her bag and this she somehow managed to wrap around the end of my tail. 'You'll be all right now,' she said. 'Just try to forget about it. Did you really manage to pour the whole bottle into their soup?'

'Every drop,' I said. 'Do you think you could put me where I can watch them?'

'Yes,' she answered. 'My handbag is on your own empty chair beside me. I'm going to pop you in there now and you can peep out as long as you are careful not to be seen. Bruno is there as well, but take no notice of him. I gave him a roll to eat and that's keeping him busy for a while.'

Her hand closed around me and I was lifted off her lap and transferred to the handbag. 'Hello, Bruno,' I said.

'This is a great roll,' he said, nibbling away in the bottom of the bag. 'But I wish there was butter on it.'

I peered over the top of the handbag. I could see the witches quite clearly sitting at their two long tables in the centre of the room. They had finished their soup now, and the waiters were clearing away the plates. My grandmother had lit up one of her disgusting black cigars and was puffing smoke over everything. All around us the summer-holiday guests in this rather grand hotel were babbling away and tucking into their suppers. About half of them were old people with walking-sticks, but there were also plenty of families with a husband, a wife and several children. They were all well-to-do people. You had to be if you wanted to stay in the Hotel Magnificent.

'That's her, Grandmamma!' I whispered. 'That's The Grand High Witch!'

'I know!' my grandmother whispered back. 'She's the tiny one in black sitting at the head of the nearest table!'

'She could kill you!' I whispered. 'She could kill anyone in this room with her white-hot sparks!'

'Look out!' my grandmother whispered. 'The waiter's coming!'

I popped down out of sight and I heard William saying, 'Your roast lamb, madam. And which vegetable would you like? Peas or carrots?'

'Carrots, please,' my grandmother said. 'But no potatoes.'

I heard the carrots being dished out. There was a pause. Then my grandmother's voice was whispering, 'It's all right. He's gone.' I popped my head up again. 'Surely no one will notice my little head sticking out like this?' I whispered.

'No,' she answered. 'I don't suppose they will. *My* problem is I've got to talk to you without moving my lips.'

'You're doing beautifully,' I said.

'I've counted the witches,' she said. 'There aren't nearly as many as you thought. You were just guessing, weren't you, when you said two hundred?'

'It just *seemed* like two hundred,' I said.

'I was wrong, too,' my grandmother said. 'I thought there were a lot more witches than this in England.'

'How many are there?' I asked.

'Eighty-four,' she said.

'There *were* eighty-five,' I said. 'But one of them got fried.'

At that moment, I caught sight of Mr Jenkins, Bruno's father, heading straight for our table. 'Look out, Grandmamma!' I whispered. 'Here comes Bruno's father!'

Chapter Nineteen

MR JENKINS AND HIS SON

Mr Jenkins came striding up to our table with a very purposeful look on his face.

'Where is that grandson of yours?' he said to my grandmother. He spoke rudely and looked very angry.

My grandmother put on her frostiest look, but didn't answer him.

'My guess is that he and my son Bruno are up to some devilment,' Mr Jenkins went on. 'Bruno hasn't turned up for his supper and it takes a lot to make that boy miss his food!'

'I must admit he has a very healthy appetite,' my grandmother said.

'My feeling is that *you're* in on this as well,' Mr Jenkins said. 'I don't know who the devil you are and I don't much care, but you played a nasty trick on me and my wife this afternoon. You put a dirty little mouse on the table. That makes me think all three of you are up to something. So if you know where Bruno's hiding, kindly tell me at once.'

'That was no trick I played on you,' my grandmother said. 'That mouse I tried to give you was your own little boy, Bruno. I was being kind to you. I was trying to restore him to the bosom of his family. You refused to take him in.'

'What the blazes do you mean, madam?' shouted Mr Jenkins. 'My son isn't a *mouse*!' His black moustache was jumping up and down like crazy as he spoke. 'Come on, woman! Where is he? Out with it!'

The family at the table nearest to us had all stopped eating and were staring at Mr Jenkins. My grandmother sat there puffing away calmly at her black cigar. 'I can well understand your anger, Mr Jenkins,' she said. 'Any other English father would be just as cross as you are. But over in Norway where I come from, we are quite used to these sorts of happenings. We have learnt to accept them as part of everyday life.'

'You must be mad, woman!' cried Mr Jenkins. 'Where is Bruno? If you don't tell me at once I shall summon the police!'

'Bruno is a mouse,' my grandmother said, calm as ever.

'He most certainly is *not* a mouse!' shouted Mr Jenkins.

'Oh yes I am!' Bruno said, poking his head up out of the handbag.

Mr Jenkins leapt about three feet into the air.

'Hello, Dad,' Bruno said. He had a silly sort of mousy grin on his face.

Mr Jenkins's mouth dropped open so wide I could see the gold fillings in his back teeth.

'Don't worry, Dad,' Bruno went on. 'It's not as bad as all that. Just so long as the cat doesn't get me.'

'B-B-Bruno!' stammered Mr Jenkins.

'No more school!' said Bruno, grinning a broad and asinine mouse-grin. 'No more homework! I shall live in the kitchen cupboard and feast on raisins and honey!'

'B-b-but B-B-Bruno!' stammered Mr Jenkins again. 'H-how did this happen?' The poor man had no wind left in his sails at all.

'Witches,' my grandmother said. 'The witches did it.'

'I can't have a mouse for a son!' shrieked Mr Jenkins.

'You've got one,' my grandmother said. 'Be nice to him, Mr Jenkins.'

'Mrs Jenkins will go crazy!' yelled Mr Jenkins. 'She can't stand the things!'

'She'll just have to get used to him,' my grandmother said. 'I hope you don't keep a cat in the house.'

'We do! We do!' cried Mr Jenkins. 'Topsy is my wife's favourite creature!'

'Then you'll just have to get rid of Topsy,' my grandmother said. 'Your son is more important than your cat.'

'He certainly is!' Bruno shouted from inside the handbag. 'You tell Mum she's got to get rid of Topsy before I go home!'

By now half the Dining-Room was watching our little group. Knives and forks and spoons had been put down and all over the place heads were turning round to stare at Mr Jenkins as he stood there spluttering and shouting. They couldn't see either Bruno or me and they were wondering what all the fuss was about.

'By the way,' my grandmother said, 'would you like to know who did this to him?' There was a mischievous little smile on her face and I could see that she was about to get Mr Jenkins into trouble.

'Who?' he cried. 'Who did it?'

'That woman over there,' my grandmother said. 'The small one in a black dress at the head of the long table.'

'She's RSPCC!' cried Mr Jenkins. 'She's the Chairwoman!'

'No, she's not,' my grandmother said. 'She's The Grand High Witch Of All The World.'

'You mean *she* did it, that skinny little woman over there!' shouted Mr Jenkins, pointing at her with a long finger. 'By gad, I'll have my lawyers on to her for this! I'll make her pay through the nose!'

'I wouldn't do anything rash,' my grandmother said to him. 'That woman has magic powers. She might decide to turn *you* into something even sillier than a mouse. A cockroach perhaps.'

'Turn *me* into a *cockroach*!' shouted Mr Jenkins, puffing out his chest. 'I'd like to see her try!' He swung around and started marching across the Dining-Room towards The Grand High Witch's table. My grandmother and I watched him. Bruno had jumped up on to our table and was also watching his father. Practically everyone in the Dining-Room was watching Mr Jenkins now. I stayed where I was, peeping out of my grandmother's handbag. I thought it might be wiser to stay put.

Chapter Twenty

THE TRIUMPH

M r Jenkins had not gone more than a few paces towards The Grand High Witch's table when a piercing scream rose high above all the other noises in the room, and at the same moment I saw The Grand High Witch go shooting up into the air!

Now she was standing on her chair, still screaming . . .

Now she was on the table-top, waving her arms . . .

'What on earth's happening, Grandmamma?'

'Wait!' my grandmother said. 'Keep quiet and watch.'

Suddenly all the other witches, more than eighty of them, were beginning to scream and jump up out of their seats as though spikes were being stuck into their bottoms. Some were standing on chairs, some were up on the tables and all of them were wiggling about and waving their arms in the most extraordinary manner.

Then, all at once, they became quiet.

Then they stiffened. Every single witch stood there as stiff and silent as a corpse.

The whole room became deathly still.

'They're shrinking, Grandmamma!' I said. 'They're shrinking just like I did!'

'I know they are,' my grandmother said.

'It's the Mouse-Maker!' I cried. 'Look! Some of them are growing fur on their faces! Why is it working so quickly, Grandmamma?'

'I'll tell you why,' my grandmother said. 'Because all of them

have had massive overdoses, just like you. It's thrown the alarm-clock right out of whack!'

Everyone in the Dining-Room was standing up now to get a better view. People were moving closer. They were beginning to crowd round the two long tables. My grandmother lifted Bruno and me up so that we wouldn't miss any of the fun. In her excitement, she jumped up on to her chair so that she could see over the heads of the crowd.

In another few seconds, all the witches had completely disappeared and the tops of the two long tables were swarming with small brown mice.

All over the Dining-Room women were screaming and strong men were turning white in the face and shouting, 'It's crazy! This can't happen! Let's get the heck out of here quick!' Waiters were attacking the mice with chairs and wine-bottles and anything else that came to hand. I saw a chef in a tall white hat rushing out from the kitchen brandishing a frying-pan, and another one just behind *him* was wielding a carving-knife above his head, and everyone was yelling, 'Mice! Mice! Mice! We must get rid of the mice!' Only the children in the room were really enjoying it. They all seemed to know instinctively that something good was going on right there in front of them, and they were clapping and cheering and laughing like mad.

'It's time to go,' my grandmother said. 'Our work is done.' She got down off her chair and picked up her handbag and slung it over her arm. She had me in her right hand and Bruno in her left. 'Bruno,' she said, 'the time has come to restore you to the famous bosom of your family.'

'My mum's not very crazy about mice,' Bruno said.

'So I noticed,' my grandmother said. 'She'll just have to get used to you, won't she?'

It was not difficult to find Mr and Mrs Jenkins. You could hear Mrs Jenkins's shrill voice all over the room. 'Herbert!' it was screaming. 'Herbert, get me out of here! There's mice everywhere! They'll go up my skirts!' She had her arms high up around her husband and from where I was she seemed to be swinging from his neck.

My grandmother advanced upon them and thrust Bruno into Mr Jenkins's hand. 'Here's your little boy,' she said. 'He needs to go on a diet.'

'Hi, Dad!' Bruno said. 'Hi, Mum!'

Mrs Jenkins screamed even louder. My grandmother, with me in her hand, turned and marched out of the room. She went straight across the hotel lobby and out through the front entrance into the open air.

Outside it was a lovely warm evening and I could hear the waves breaking on the beach just across the road from the hotel.

'Is there a taxi here?' my grandmother said to the tall doorman in his green uniform.

'Certainly, madam,' he said, and he put two fingers into his mouth and blew a long shrill whistle. I watched him with envy. For weeks I had been trying to whistle like that but I hadn't succeeded once. Now I never would.

The taxi came. The driver was an oldish man with a thick black drooping moustache. The moustache hung over his mouth like the roots of some plant. 'Where to, madam?' he asked. Suddenly, he caught sight of me, a little mouse, nestling in my grandmother's hand. 'Blimey!' he said. 'What's that?'

'It's my grandson,' my grandmother said. 'Drive us to the station, please.'

'I always liked mice,' the old taxi-driver said. 'I used to keep 'undreds of 'em when I was a boy. Mice is the fastest breeders in the world, did you know that, ma'am? So if 'ee's your grandson, then I reckon you'll be having a few *great*-grandsons to go with 'im in a couple of weeks' time!'

'Drive us to the station, please,' my grandmother said, looking prim.

'Yes, ma'am,' he said. 'Right away.'

My grandmother got into the back of the taxi and sat down and put me on her lap.

'Are we going home?' I asked her.

'Yes,' she answered. 'Back to Norway.'

'Hooray!' I cried. 'Oh, hooray, hooray, hooray!'

'I thought you'd like that,' she said.

'But what about our luggage?'

'Who cares about luggage?' she said.

The taxi was driving through the streets of Bournemouth and this was the time of day when the pavements were crowded with holiday-makers all wandering about aimlessly with nothing to do.

'How are you feeling, my darling?' my grandmother said.

'Fine,' I said. 'Quite marvellous.'

She began stroking the fur on the back of my neck with one finger. 'We have accomplished great feats today,' she said.

'It's been terrific,' I said. 'Absolutely terrific.'

Chapter Twenty-One

THE HEART OF A MOUSE

It was lovely to be back in Norway once again in my grandmother's fine old house. But now that I was so small, everything looked different and it took me quite a while to find my way around. Mine was a world of carpets and table-legs and chair-legs and the little crannies behind large pieces of furniture. A closed door could not be opened and nothing could be reached that was on a table.

But after a few days, my grandmother began to invent gadgets for me in order to make life a bit easier. She got a carpenter to put together a number of slim tall stepladders and she placed one of these against each table in the house so that I could climb up whenever I wanted to. She herself invented a wonderful door-opening device made out of wires and springs and pulleys, with heavy weights dangling on cords, and soon every door in the house had a door-opener on it. All I had to do was to press my front paws on to a tiny wooden platform and hey presto, a spring would stretch and a weight would drop and the door would swing open.

Next, she rigged up an equally ingenious system whereby I could switch on the light whenever I entered a room at night. I cannot explain how it worked because I know nothing about electricity, but there was a little button let into the floor near the door in every room in the house, and when I pressed the button gently with one paw, the light would come on. When I pressed it a second time, the light would go off again.

My grandmother made me a tiny toothbrush, using a matchstick for the handle, and into this she stuck little bits of bristle that she had snipped off one of her hairbrushes. 'You *must* not get any holes in your teeth,' she said. 'I can't take a *mouse* to a dentist! He'd think I was crazy!'

'It's funny,' I said, 'but ever since I became a mouse I've hated the taste of sweets and chocolate. So I don't think I'll get any holes.'

'You are still going to brush your teeth after every meal,' my grandmother said. And I did.

For a bath-tub she gave me a silver sugar-basin, and I bathed in it every night before going to bed. She allowed no one else into the house, not even a servant or a cook. We kept entirely to ourselves and we were very happy in each other's company.

One evening, as I lay on my grandmother's lap in front of the fire, she said to me, 'I wonder what happened to that little Bruno.'

'I wouldn't be surprised if his father gave him to the hall-porter to drown in the fire-bucket,' I answered.

'I'm afraid you may be right,' my grandmother said. 'The poor little thing.'

We were silent for a few minutes, my grandmother puffing away at her black cigar while I dozed comfortably in the warmth.

'Can I ask you something, Grandmamma?' I said.

'Ask me anything you like, my darling.'

'How long does a mouse live?'

'Ah,' she said. 'I've been waiting for you to ask me that.'

There was a silence. She sat there smoking away and gazing at the fire.

'Well,' I said. 'How long *do* we live, us mice?'

'I have been reading about mice,' she said. 'I have been trying to find out everything I can about them.'

'Go on then, Grandmamma. Why don't you tell me?'

'If you really want to know,' she said, 'I'm afraid a mouse doesn't live for a very long time.'

'How long?' I asked.

'Well, an *ordinary* mouse only lives for about three years,' she said. 'But you are not an ordinary mouse. You are a mouse-person, and that is a very different matter.'

'How different?' I asked. 'How long does a mouse-person live, Grandmamma?'

'Longer,' she said. 'Much longer.'

'A mouse-person will almost certainly live for three times as long as an ordinary mouse,' my grandmother said. 'About nine years.'

'Good!' I cried. 'That's great! It's the best news I've ever had!'

'Why do you say that?' she asked, surprised.

'Because I would never want to live longer than you,' I said. 'I couldn't stand being looked after by anybody else.'

There was a short silence. She had a way of fondling me behind the ears with the tip of one finger. It felt lovely.

'How old are *you*, Grandmamma?' I asked.

'I'm eighty-six,' she said.

'Will you live another eight or nine years?'

'I might,' she said. 'With a bit of luck.'

'You've got to,' I said. 'Because by then I'll be a very old mouse and you'll be a very old grandmother and soon after that we'll both die together.'

'That would be perfect,' she said.

I had a little doze after that. I just shut my eyes and thought of nothing and felt at peace with the world.

'Would you like me to tell you something about yourself that is very interesting?' my grandmother said.

'Yes please, Grandmamma,' I said, without opening my eyes.

'I couldn't believe it at first, but apparently it's quite true,' she said.

'What is it?' I asked.

'The heart of a mouse,' she said, 'and that means *your* heart, is beating at the rate of *five hundred times a minute*! Isn't that amazing?'

'That's not possible,' I said, opening my eyes wide.

'It's as true as I'm sitting here,' she said. 'It's a sort of a miracle.'

'That's nearly nine beats every second!' I cried, working it out in my head.

'Correct,' she said. 'Your heart is going so fast it's impossible to hear the separate beats. All one hears is a soft humming sound.'

She was wearing a lace dress and the lace kept tickling my nose. I had to rest my head on my front paws.

'Have *you* ever heard my heart humming away, Grandmamma?' I asked her.

'Often,' she said. 'I hear it when you are lying very close to me on the pillow at night.'

The two of us remained silent in front of the fire for a long time after that, thinking about these wonderful things.

'My darling,' she said at last, 'are you sure you don't mind being a mouse for the rest of your life?'

'I don't mind at all,' I said. 'It doesn't matter who you are or what you look like so long as somebody loves you.'

Chapter Twenty-Two

IT'S OFF TO WORK WE GO!

For supper that evening my grandmother had a plain omelette and one slice of bread. I had a piece of that brown Norwegian goats'-milk cheese known as *gjetost* which I had loved even when I was a boy. We ate in front of the fire, my grandmother in her armchair and me on the table with my cheese on a small plate.

'Grandmamma,' I said, 'now that we have done away with The Grand High Witch, will all the other witches in the world gradually disappear?'

'I'm quite sure they won't,' she answered.

I stopped chewing and stared at her. 'But they *must*!' I cried. 'Surely they must!'

'I'm afraid not,' she said.

'But if she's not there any longer how are they going to get all the money they need? And who is going to give them orders and jazz them up at the Annual Meetings and invent all their magic formulas for them?'

'When a queen bee dies, there is always another queen in the hive ready to take her place,' my grandmother said. 'It's the same with witches. In the great headquarters where The Grand High Witch lives, there is always another Grand High Witch waiting in the wings to take over should anything happen.'

'Oh no!' I cried. 'That means everything we did was for nothing! Have I become a mouse for nothing at all?'

'We saved the children of England,' she said. 'I don't call that nothing.'

'I know, I know!' I cried. 'But that's not nearly good enough! I felt sure that all the witches of the world would slowly fade away after we had got rid of their leader! Now you tell me that everything is going to go on just the same as before!'

'Not exactly as before,' my grandmother said. 'For instance, there are no longer any witches in England. That's quite a triumph, isn't it?'

'But what about the rest of the world?' I cried. 'What about America and France and Holland and Germany? And what about Norway?'

'You must not think I have been sitting back and doing nothing these last few days,' she said. 'I have been giving a great deal of thought and time to that particular problem.'

I was looking up at her face when she said this, and all at once I noticed that a little secret smile was beginning to spread slowly around her eyes and the corners of her mouth. 'Why are you smiling, Grandmamma?' I asked her.

'I have some rather interesting news for you,' she said.

'What news?'

'Shall I tell it to you right from the beginning?'

'Yes please,' I said. 'I like good news.'

She had finished her omelette, and I had had enough of my cheese. She wiped her lips with a napkin and said, 'As soon as we arrived back in Norway, I picked up the telephone and made a call to England.'

'Who in England, Grandmamma?'

'To the Chief of Police in Bournemouth, my darling. I told him I was the Chief of Police for the whole of Norway and that I was interested in the peculiar happenings that had taken place recently

in the Hotel Magnificent.'

'Now hang on a sec, Grandmamma,' I said. 'There's no way an English policeman is going to believe that *you* are the Head of the Norwegian Police.'

'I am very good at imitating a man's voice,' she said. 'Of course he believed me. The policeman in Bournemouth was honoured to get a call from the Chief of Police for the whole of Norway.'

'So what did you ask him?'

'I asked him for the name and address of the lady who had been living in Room 454 in the Hotel Magnificent, the one who disappeared.'

'You mean The Grand High Witch!' I cried.

'Yes, my darling.'

'And did he give it to you?'

'Naturally he gave it to me. One policeman will always help another policeman.'

'By golly, you've got a nerve, Grandmamma!'

'I wanted her address,' my grandmother said.

'But did he *know* her address?'

'He did indeed. They had found her passport in her room and her address was in it. It was also in the hotel register. Everyone who stays in a hotel has to put a name and address in the book.'

'But surely The Grand High Witch wouldn't have put her *real* name and address in the hotel register?' I said.

'Why ever not?' my grandmother said. 'Nobody in the world had the faintest idea who she was except the other witches. Wherever she went, people simply knew her as a nice lady. *You*, my darling, and *you alone*, were the only non-witch ever to see her with her mask off. Even in her home district, in the village where she lived, people knew her as a kindly and very wealthy Baroness who gave large sums of money to charity. I have checked up on that.'

I was getting excited now. 'And that address you got, Grandmamma, that must have been the secret headquarters of The Grand High Witch.'

'It still is,' my grandmother said. 'And that will be where the new Grand High Witch is certain to be living at this very moment with her retinue of special Assistant Witches. Important rulers are always surrounded by a large retinue of assistants.'

'Where is her headquarters, Grandmamma?' I cried. 'Tell me quick where it is!'

'It is a Castle,' my grandmother said. 'And the fascinating thing is that in that Castle will be all the names and addresses of all the witches in the world! How else could a Grand High Witch run her business? How else could she summon the witches of the various countries to their Annual Meetings?'

'Where is the Castle, Grandmamma?' I cried impatiently. 'Which country? Tell me quick!'

'Guess,' she said.

'Norway!' I cried.

'Right first time!' she answered. 'High up in the mountains above a small village.'

This was thrilling news. I did a little dance of excitement on the table-top. My grandmother was getting pretty worked up herself

and now she heaved herself out of her chair and began pacing up and down the room, thumping the carpet with her stick.

'So we have work to do, you and I!' she cried out. 'We have a great task ahead of us! Thank heavens you are a mouse! A mouse can go anywhere! All I'll have to do is put you down somewhere near The Grand High Witch's Castle and you will very easily be able to get inside it and creep around looking and listening to your heart's content!'

'I will! I will!' I answered. 'No one will ever see me! Moving about in a big Castle will be child's play compared with going into a crowded kitchen full of cooks and waiters!'

'You could spend *days* in there if necessary!' my grandmother cried. In her excitement she was waving her stick all over the place, and suddenly she knocked over a tall and very beautiful vase that went crashing on to the floor and smashed into a million pieces. 'Forget it,' she said. 'It's only Ming. You could spend *weeks* in that Castle if you wanted to and they'd never know you were there! I myself would get a room in the village and you could sneak out of the Castle and have supper with me every night and tell me what was going on.'

'I could! I could!' I cried out. 'And inside the Castle I could go snooping around simply everywhere!'

'But your main job, of course,' my grandmother said, 'would be to destroy every witch in the place. That really *would* be the end of the whole organization!'

'*Me* destroy *them*?' I cried. 'How could I do that?'

'Can't you guess?' she said.

'Tell me,' I said.

'Mouse-Maker!' my grandmother shouted. 'Formula 86 Delayed Action Mouse-Maker all over again! You will feed it to everyone in the Castle by putting drops of it into their food! You do remember the recipe, don't you?'

'Every bit of it!' I answered. 'You mean we're going to make it ourselves?'

'Why not?' she cried. 'If *they* can make it, so can we! It's just a question of knowing what goes into it!'

'Who's going to climb up the tall trees to get the gruntles' eggs?' I asked her.

'I will!' she cried. 'I'll do it myself! There's plenty of life in this old dog yet!'

'I think I'd better do that part of it, Grandmamma. You might come a cropper.'

'Those are just details!' she cried, waving her stick again. 'We shall let nothing stand in our way!'

'And what happens after that?' I asked her. 'After the new Grand High Witch and everyone else in the Castle have been turned into mice?'

'Then the Castle will be completely empty and I shall come in and join you and . . .'

'Wait!' I cried. 'Hold on, Grandmamma! I've just had a nasty thought!'

'What nasty thought?' she said.

'When the Mouse-Maker turned *me* into a mouse,' I said, 'I didn't become just any old ordinary mouse that you catch with mouse-traps. I became a talking thinking intelligent mouse-person who wouldn't go *near* a mouse-trap!'

My grandmother stopped dead in her tracks. She already knew what was coming next.

'Therefore,' I went on, 'if we use the Mouse-Maker to turn the new Grand High Witch and all the other witches in the Castle into mice, the whole place will be swarming with very clever, very nasty, very dangerous talking thinking mouse-witches! They'll all be witches in mouse's clothing. And that,' I added, 'could be very horrible indeed.'

'By golly, you're right!' she cried. 'That never occurred to me!'

'I couldn't possibly take on a castleful of mouse-witches,' I said.

'Nor could I,' she said. 'They'd have to be got rid of at once. They'd have to be smashed and bashed and chopped up into little pieces exactly as they were in the Hotel Magnificent.'

'I'm not doing that,' I said. 'I couldn't anyway. I don't think you could either, Grandmamma. And mouse-traps wouldn't be the slightest use. By the way,' I added, 'The Grand High Witch who did me in was wrong about mouse-traps, wasn't she?'

'Yes, yes,' my grandmother said impatiently. 'But I'm not concerned with *that* Grand High Witch. She's been chopped up long ago by the hotel chef. It's the *new* Grand High Witch we've got to deal with now, the one up in the Castle, and all her assistants. A Grand High Witch is bad enough when she's disguised as a lady, but just think of what she could do if she were a mouse! She could go anywhere!'

'I've got it!' I shouted, leaping about a foot in the air. 'I've got the answer!'

'Tell me!' my grandmother snapped.

'The answer is CATS!' I shouted. 'Bring on the cats!'

My grandmother stared at me. Then a great grin spread over her face and she shouted, 'It's brilliant! Absolutely brilliant!'

'Shove half-a-dozen cats into that Castle,' I cried, 'and they'll kill every mouse in the place in five minutes, I don't care how clever they are!'

'You're a magician!' my grandmother shouted, starting to wave her stick about once again.

'Look out for the vases, Grandmamma!'

'To heck with the vases!' she shouted. 'I'm so thrilled I don't care if I break the lot!'

'Just one thing,' I said. 'You've got to make absolutely sure I'm well out of the way myself before you put the cats in.'

'That's a promise,' she said.

'What will we do after the cats have killed all the mice?' I asked her.

'I'll take all the cats back to the village and then you and I will have the Castle completely to ourselves.'

'And then?' I said.

'Then we shall go through the records and get the names and addresses of all the witches in the whole wide world!'

'And after that?' I said, quivering with excitement.

'After that, my darling, the greatest task of all will begin for you and me! We shall pack our bags and go travelling all over the world! In every country we visit, we shall seek out the houses where the witches are living! We shall find each house, one by one, and having found it, you will creep inside and leave your little drops of deadly Mouse-Maker in the bread, or the cornflakes, or the rice-pudding or whatever food you see lying about. It will be a triumph, my darling! A colossal unbeatable triumph. We shall do it entirely by ourselves, just you and me! That will be our work for the rest of our lives!'

My grandmother picked me up off the table and kissed me on the nose. 'Oh, my goodness me, we're going to be busy these next few weeks and months and years!' she cried.

'I think we are,' I said. 'But what fun and excitement it's going to be!'

'You can say that again!' my grandmother cried, giving me another kiss. 'I can't wait to get started!'

STORIES ARE GOOD FOR YOU.

Roald Dahl said,
*'If you have good thoughts, they will shine
out of your face like sunbeams and you
will always look lovely.'*

We believe in doing good things.
That's why ten per cent of all Roald Dahl income*
goes to our charity partners. We have supported
causes including: specialist children's nurses, grants for
families in need, and educational outreach programmes.
Thank you for helping us to sustain this vital work.

Find out more at roalddahl.com

The Roald Dahl Charitable Trust is a registered UK charity (no. 1119330).
* All author payments and royalty income net of third-party commissions.

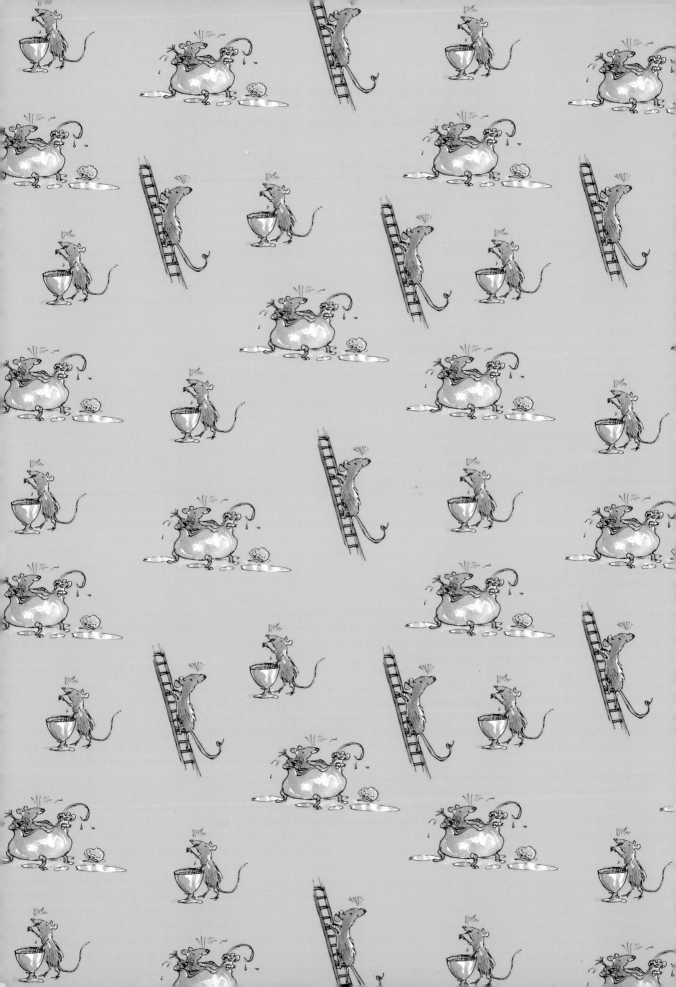